Jason's bare foot hit the chilly flesh, and sent him sprawling onto the cold, wet sand. His mind spun, shock filling his body. What had he tripped over? It couldn't have been—

He scrambled up and turned around, praying he'd been wrong about what he'd seen. But the girl's body still lay there. Face down. Her flesh cold and blue.

CPR, Jason ordered himself. *Move, go!*

He dropped to his knees next to the girl and tried to roll her onto her back, but she felt heavy, waterlogged. A wave splashed onto the shore, its undertow pulling her out of his grasp. Jason felt the setting sun hot upon the back of his neck as he reached for her cold arm again.

He waited for the next wave and used the thrust of the water to help him roll her over. Her blank eyes stared up at him.

It was too late for Jason to help her. Too late for anyone.

She was dead.

VAMPIRE BEACH

Don't miss any of the titles in this edgy series:

Book One: Bloodlust

Coming soon:

Book Two: Initiation

VAMPIRE BEACH

Bloodlust

Alex Duval

RED FOX BOOKS

VAMPIRE BEACH: BLOODLUST
A RED FOX BOOK 978 1 862 301948 (from January 2007)
1 862 30194 8

First published in Great Britain by Red Fox,
an imprint of Random House Children's Books

This edition published 2006

1 3 5 7 9 10 8 6 4 2

Papers used by Random House Children's Books are natural, recyclable products
made from wood grown in sustainable forests. The manufacturing processes
conform to the environmental regulations of the country of origin.

Set in 12/16pt Minion by
FalconOast Graphic Art Ltd.

Red Fox Books are published by Random House Children's Books,
61–63 Uxbridge Road, London W5 5SA,
a division of The Random House Group Ltd,
in Australia by Random House Australia (Pty) Ltd,
20 Alfred Street, Milsons Point, Sydney, NSW 2061, Australia,
in New Zealand by Random House New Zealand Ltd,
18 Poland Road, Glenfield, Auckland 10, New Zealand,
and in South Africa by Random House (Pty) Ltd,
Isle of Houghton, Corner Boundary Road & Carse O'Gowrie,
Houghton 2198, South Africa

THE RANDOM HOUSE GROUP Limited Reg. No. 954009
www.kidsatrandomhouse.co.uk

A CIP catalogue record for this book is available from the British Library.

Printed and bound in Great Britain by
Cox & Wyman Ltd, Reading, Berkshire

For Amber Caravéo –
there would be no Vampire Beach
without you

Special thanks to Laura Burns & Melinda Metz

ONE

Malibu.

Jason Freeman took a deep breath of the fresh California air. He *lived* in Malibu now. This was him, driving his VW Karmann Cabriolet Beetle down the Pacific Coast Highway. The thought was as blinding as the sun on the ocean, as dazzling as the white sand stretching out alongside the car – *right* alongside the car. He could pull over and be down there in—

'How insane is that house?'

Jason reluctantly dragged his gaze away from the . . . the *Malibu*, and glanced at the house his younger sister, Danielle, was pointing to. She'd pulled her sunglasses down for a better look, and her gray eyes were wide with curiosity.

'It has a tennis court!' she declared. 'And I bet that glass dome is for an indoor pool. They don't let you see much, do they? All those trellises and flowers.' Dani glanced over her shoulder as they drove by, trying to eye-TiVO every detail. 'That new job of Dad's, the un-pass-by-able job, the one I had to leave all my friends for? It pays a gazillion dollars. Why aren't we living in a place like that?'

'Places like that cost multiple gazillions,' Jason told her. 'Besides, we have a pool at the new house.'

'An *outdoor* pool,' Dani complained. But Jason could hear a hint of amusement in her voice. The idea of complaining about anything in this town was ridiculous.

'Don't knock the pool. It's a lovely kidney shape, with colored tile detailing,' Jason said, quoting the real-estate agent with a wry smile.

Dani adjusted her Oliver Peoples sunglasses that had been a gift from their Aunt Bianca: the aunt who – aside from having impeccable fashion sense – had also first mentioned the new job to their dad *and* helped find their new house.

'True. But the pool doesn't make up for being dragged halfway across the country two weeks before junior year,' Dani said flatly.

Jason sighed. He knew the leaving-all-her-friends part of the situation had really upset Danielle. She'd had at least thirty 'best friends' back in Michigan, and she hadn't wanted to part with any of them.

'Hey, so I heard about this guy called the Surf Rabbi,' he said, trying to get Dani's mind off her homesickness. 'He's an actual rabbi. He's like fifty years old, and he gives surfing lessons: spiritual surfing lessons. He's all about, I don't know, giving yourself over to the water, or something. He teaches in Malibu.'

'Hmm,' Dani managed.

Jason shot a look at the surfers already out in the ocean. Sweet. He couldn't wait to get out there himself. But he might need to pay a visit to the rabbi first, seeing as he'd never set foot on a board.

The lifeguard stations on their long wooden legs reminded him of another thing he needed to do. He had to find out where to apply for a job as a guard. That was seriously on the top ten list of things to do now that he was living in California, right after joining a gym. He figured he had a decent shot at getting a lifeguard job, since he'd been on the swim team back home, and he'd already taken a lifesaving course.

'Jeans!' Dani gasped as they neared the school gates.

'Huh?' Jason queried.

'I have to change,' Dani said, as if that was actually an explanation. Jason raised his eyebrows. She rushed on. 'Those girls we just passed were all wearing designer jeans!' She shook her head, her chin-length auburn hair flying around her face. 'And I'm in a skirt. I'm not dressed right.'

Jason sighed. 'We don't have time for you to change. We just got here. Besides, what you're wearing is fine,' he assured her.

Danielle pulled out a brush and whipped it through her hair. 'It's different for you. You're a guy. You have the vintage bug. You have the blond hair/blue eyes combo. You look like you could be the son of Jude Law and . . . and somebody not so British. Nobody's going to care what you're wearing.'

'And you're the only one who cares what *you're* wearing!' Jason countered. 'You look great. You always do. Chill out, Dani.'

Jason swung the car into the parking lot of DeVere High. DeVere, as in DeVere Heights: the gated complex where they now lived. And DeVere University. And DeVere Museum of Modern Art. And DeVere Library. And DeVere Athletic Complex, et cetera, et cetera and et cetera. He killed the engine and opened the car door.

Dani remained motionless. Her gray eyes were filled with apprehension behind her shades. She hated change. She always had. She'd actually insisted on moving every single Narnia book she'd ever owned across the country, even though she hadn't read them for years. She seemed to think that the world would end if she didn't have them stuffed in her closet in Malibu, just the way she'd had them stuffed in her closet in Michigan.

Jason had handed out his belongings left and right. He wanted to start clean here. No mooning over his past life, no calling his old friends every five minutes, no thinking about Michigan like it had been some kind of paradise. He wished he could give Dani a transfusion of some of his excitement. They were in Malibu now. Life was going to change. And Jason wanted it to. In Fraser, the suburb where he'd lived since birth, he had been able to see every day, every week, every month stretching out in front of him. Not bad. But boring. Here he had no idea what was going to happen – and it was a total rush!

'Listen. You had more friends than any other human at our old school,' Jason reminded his sister. 'It's not going to be any different here.' He climbed out of the car. The bug looked like a toy among all the hellaciously big H2s and Range Rovers that filled the lot. Still, Jason spotted at least ten new Mercedes SLK convertibles and several other vintage cars like his own. Not everyone was an SUV freak.

He glanced at Dani. She was still in the car. A couple of girls around his sister's age – sixteen – walked by, laughing and gossiping to each other just like girls everywhere. 'They don't seem so evil,' Jason pointed out.

With a sigh, Dani climbed from the car and gave the girls a once-over. 'They definitely wouldn't survive a winter in Michigan,' she said at last.

'There's the old Dani attitude,' Jason joked. He smiled as he led the way to the main building. It looked nothing like a school – an art gallery, maybe, a mansion or a spa, sure, but not a school. It had arches and parapets and red roof tiles. A bell tower rose up from one side. And a wide porch wrapped around the second floor.

They stepped through the largest archway and found themselves in a central courtyard with a manicured lawn in the middle, surrounded by palm trees. Jason still wasn't used to seeing palms all over the place. And flowers grew like weeds out here, not in neat little gardens, but everywhere – on the medians of the freeways, on the sides of buildings; he'd even seen some growing around the trunks of palm trees.

'I'm this way,' he announced, stopping in a cool, dim walkway next to the courtyard. Stone steps led up to a side door, and his school map showed him that his first class should be right inside. He looked at the class schedule Dani was clutching so tightly that the blood had drained from her fingers, leaving them bone white. 'You're over there . . .' he added, nodding in the opposite direction, where another set of stairs led into the wing across the courtyard.

'Yep,' Dani replied shortly. She looked terrified at the prospect of going it alone.

'Look, just make it through this first week. You can do that,' Jason told her encouragingly.

'And then what?'

He tried to think of something that would keep her going. 'I'll take you to the movies on Saturday,' he suggested. 'Even if it means sitting through a chick flick!'

Dani laughed a little shakily. 'OK.' She took a deep breath. 'See ya after.'

Jason nodded. 'I'll be at the car,' he said, and headed away from her, into what he hoped would be . . . the unexpected.

Nothing unexpected in the first three periods, Jason thought as he joined the cafeteria food line. Well, nothing if you didn't count the fact that all the kids looked as if they had dermatologists and orthodontists and any other –ontists and –ologists that kept you perfect. And the fact that the cafeteria was mostly taken up by a terrace overlooking the Pacific – which was kind of a surprise. He couldn't wait to grab his food and get out there.

Somehow, when he moved here, Jason had thought his life would . . . well, *start*. And so far, school was still school. Beautiful. But still just school.

'Would you hand me the last green Borba?'

Jason turned toward the voice. And instantly felt as if every vein, artery and capillary in his body had caught fire. He could *feel* the blood rushing through them – pulsing, throbbing. He felt alive in a way he never had before. And life was full of possibility.

The girl who stood there was the most beautiful thing he had ever seen, hair spilling down over her shoulders like a black waterfall, eyes almost as dark. Her lips were a little plump, as if they were full of something sweet, filling Jason with an almost overwhelming desire to kiss her. It struck him that he had never found a girl so instantly desirable before.

'Green Borba?' the girl repeated.

How long had it been since she asked the first time? A second? Five? Long enough to make him look like a complete moron? Jason dragged his eyes away from her and over to the lunch counter. There was an array of sushi in front of him. But he'd never heard of a sushi called Borba. Not that he'd heard of every type of sushi in the world, but he wasn't sushi-challenged or anything.

'OK, you said it was the last one. And that it was green. One more hint, and I know I can get it,' Jason told her.

The girl shook her head and smiled. 'Oh, right. You're from a flyover.'

A 'flyover'. That didn't sound especially good.

The girl reached across Jason and picked up a green bottle of water from a shelf above the sushi. She started toward the cashier, but Jason wasn't ready for their conversation to be over.

'So, what makes green Borba different from' – he took a quick look at the other bottles of water – 'from purple or pink Borba? And which one should I be drinking?'

She looked him up and down thoughtfully. 'Some things you just have to find out for yourself,' she said with a smile. Then she gave him a half wave and walked away.

Jason stared after her. He couldn't help himself. The

tight T-shirt she wore tucked into a short cargo skirt showed off the curve of her waist followed by a long stretch of tanned legs.

He realized he was holding up the line, so he grabbed one of the waters, just to see what the deal was, slid his tray down to the burgers, acquired one with some seasoned curly fries, paid up, and headed toward that outrageous terrace.

The sun hit him full force the second he stepped out the door. It was a little windy, but the sound of the surf pounding the beach below more than made up for it. He glanced around. Stone tables in a variety of shapes dotted the terrace, most of them already taken.

'Hey, Freeman. Over here.'

Some sandy-haired guy – Alex? Adam? – from Jason's history class was waving him over with one hand and pointing a small, sleek camcorder at him with the other.

'European history,' Jason said to Sandy-haired Guy, wanting to show he remembered him, even though they hadn't actually met.

'Yep,' the guy answered, still filming. 'I'm Adam Turnball. Give me your impression of DeVere!'

'Are you making a documentary?' Jason asked.

'It's more of a Christopher Guest/Richard Linklater

semi-scripted, lots-of-improv. kind of thing,' Adam replied somewhat cryptically.

Jason glanced at the other guy who had staked out the far end of the table. He was hoping for a translation, but the guy didn't look up from his book.

'Come on. Talk to me. Anything,' Adam urged.

'Cool cars in the lot, great views.' *The hottest girl I've ever seen!* Jason silently added, then continued, 'A wide selection of chow. Speaking of which' – he sat down – 'my burger is cooling.'

'Oh, sorry.' Adam shut off the camera and turned to his pizza.

Jason twisted the top off his purple Borba and took a slug. It tasted like water with a little berry thing happening. 'Five bucks a bottle, you'd think they could throw in a little more kick!' he mumbled.

'Well, yeah, but it's not about the taste,' Adam said, his hazel eyes twinkling. 'It's about the protection.'

'What?'

'It's a prophylactic,' Adam said, nodding at the Borba with a sly smile. 'Against aging. Of course, you need to drink two a day for maximum effectiveness.'

Jason read the side of the bottle. Crap, it *was* for aging skin. Why were they selling it in a high school cafeteria? He ran his hand over his cheek. 'I heard the sun out here is very drying,' he said to Adam. 'Also, I didn't read the label.'

Adam laughed. 'So, should I pretend I don't already know where you're from, et cetera, and ask you all the normal questions?'

'I guess if you already know, it's kinda pointless,' Jason answered. '*How* do you know?'

'You live in the Heights. Everyone in Malibu knows who lives there. Movie stars, moguls, music producers, and to keep to my "m" theme, magnificent, newly successful ad execs from Michigan, like your dad. We hate you. And we all want to be you at the same time,' Adam said. 'You're all we talk about. Real-estate agents pass on the dirt, along with landscapers and interior decorators. There's a whole information infrastructure.'

'And who exactly is this *we*?' Jason asked, taking a bite of his burger.

'You know, the people from the wrong side of the tracks,' Adam replied. 'Not that there is a wrong side of the tracks in Malibu. Let's say the wrong side of the gate that leads into DeVere Heights.'

'So I'm guessing you're not mogul or movie-star spawn,' Jason said with a grin.

'I am the child of the poor but hardworking Chief of

Police,' Adam answered, so cheerfully that Jason suspected he didn't give a crap about not living in the Heights.

'Can I ask you something?' Jason ventured.

'I live to serve,' Adam quipped.

Jason shot a glance at the guy at the far end of the table. He was still reading. 'What's a flyover?'

Adam half stood up and spoke in one of those whispers that are supposed to sound like shouts. 'Hey, everybody, the new guy doesn't know what a flyover is!'

Nobody responded. Nobody even glanced at them. 'It's one of the states you fly over to get between California and New York,' he told Jason. 'You know, those two being the only worthwhile states.'

As I suspected, she basically called me a loser, Jason thought.

Adam polished off the rest of his pizza. 'So what else? Ask me anything.'

Jason wanted to ask about the girl who had turned him inside out. But he wasn't ready to be quite that pathetic – and obvious – yet. 'How about a who's-who?' he asked instead. 'I need to put some names to faces.'

'Well, there's me,' Adam said. He struck a pose.

'Adam. Turnball. Remember the name and when I'm the next Scorcese you can say you knew me back in the day.'

'I'll try to remember,' Jason joked.

'And over to our left is Luke Archer, whose position as "new boy" you are currently usurping. Hey, Luke, how long has it been?'

'A year,' Luke said without looking up.

'Huh. Time flies,' Adam replied. 'Supply an interesting factoid about yourself for the new guy, please.'

'Uh, I have a dachshund named Hans,' Luke volunteered, finally glancing up and shoving his longish blond hair out of his green eyes.

'I never knew that about you,' Adam said, but Luke had already returned to his book.

'Give me some social survival hints,' Jason said. 'Like, who's cool, who's psychotic. Basically, who should I hang with and who should I stay the hell away from?'

'Ah. That will take a while,' Adam replied, and grabbed a curly fry off Jason's plate. 'But I'll give you the *Cliffs Notes* version. You've got your two basic groups here: the normal people and the rock stars.'

'Rock stars?' Jason asked skeptically.

'I exaggerate,' Adam said cheerfully. 'What I mean is,

there are normal people – like myself. And then there are people who live in DeVere Heights – like you. Although you don't quite fit the mold. No offense.'

'What mold?' Jason asked.

'Not to sound too much like I'm describing some hideous teen soap, but DeVere kids are rich, they're beautiful, and they're painfully cool,' Adam explained.

'And I'm not?' Jason laughed, pretending to be insulted.

'Don't get me wrong, you seem decent and all. You just don't have that *je ne sais quoi* that the DeVere Heights natives possess.'

'I can live with that,' Jason replied. 'So, tell me about these rock stars. Who are they?'

'The first name you need to know is Zach Lafrenière,' Adam began. 'Mom's a writer – with an Oscar. Dad's a music producer. So, he's got good blood. And Zach cares about that crap, even though he likes to pretend he doesn't. His own credits aren't bad. Basketball star – he led us to victory last year. He's also had a little part in a movie – not one of his mom's. And he went to the senior prom with Paige Devereux, when he was still a *freshman* – now *that's* a big deal! Now that he's a senior, he's the big enchilada, as we like to say around here. Actually, only I like to say it. You probably shouldn't. You don't have enough of the ironic vibe to pull it off. Not that I'm judging you.'

'Which one is he?' Jason asked, glancing around the terrace.

'He's not here. Monsieur Lafrenière will not be joining us for a couple of weeks as he's in France with his parents,' Adam answered. 'Visiting the homelands.'

Jason tried to steer the conversation without being obvious about what exactly it was he wanted to know. 'So, who's the female equivalent of this Zach guy?' he prompted.

'Who's the woman?' Adam shook his head. 'No contest. Paige passed the It Girl torch to her little sister, Sienna. She's a senior now. Paige is off in college.'

'And where's Sienna? Hawaii?' A little too late, Jason realized that Hawaii probably wasn't a big deal when you lived in Malibu.

Adam grinned as if he could read Jason's thoughts. 'Nothing so mundane,' he joked. 'She's right over there. A couple of tables behind us. Black hair, a body that's impossible to miss . . .'

Jason knew who he'd see before he turned around, but he took a fast look anyway.

She was looking back at him, and she raised an eyebrow when she spotted the purple Borba in his hand.

Kill me now, Jason thought. He raised the bottle in a toast, trying to cover his embarrassment.

Sienna smiled – a slow, painfully sexy smile – and raised her Borba in return. Then she turned away, laughing at something one of her friends had said. And suddenly Jason felt cold, as if the sun had gone in.

'Besides Sienna and Zach, we have Brad Moreau . . .' Adam continued.

But Jason wasn't listening. All he could think about was how well her name matched up with her. Sienna. It was sexy. Exotic. Unusual. Unexpected . . .

TWO

Thank you, God, for the alphabet, Jason thought, *which led to alphabetical seating, which led to this Freeman sitting directly across the aisle from Sienna Devereux.* English was now officially his favorite class.

The teacher, Ms Hoffman, started doing the what's-expected-of-you-this-year speech. She explained what percentage of your grade came from homework or from tests or from class participation, she went through the reading list, she told them the number of papers and when they were due, and so on and so on. Jason knew he should be paying attention; English wasn't exactly his best subject. But the thing was, Sienna was so close he could smell her perfume – a mix of green apple and vanilla and the ocean. Tangy-sweet and yet somehow also mysterious.

'Jason Freeman.'

The sound of his name jerked Jason out of his

trance. The way that Ms Hoffman was looking at him made it clear that she'd just asked him a question. Everyone in the room had turned to stare at him in his moment of embarrassment, an assortment of smirks and grins on their faces. He felt a flush creep up the back of his neck, and it only got worse when he saw Sienna watching him.

'Uh, can you repeat that?' he asked. 'I'm a flyover and everyone knows we're kinda backward.'

'You're *from* a flyover,' Sienna corrected him, but she was grinning.

He winced. 'See? Backward.'

A few other kids chuckled and Ms Hoffman smiled. 'I asked if you've already studied *Macbeth*,' she said. 'That's what we'll be starting with.'

Bonus. Jason had!

He managed to keep his focus on Ms Hoffman for the rest of English. He noticed she had a pair of Peoples sunglasses hooked over her white T-shirt, just like Dani and half the other girls he'd seen today. Clearly, being tragically underpaid was not a problem for teachers at DeVere. Either that, or Ms Hoffman skipped meals in order to keep herself in eyewear. He wondered if even the janitors here wore designer shades.

When the bell rang, Jason joined the throng of

students in the hallway. Soon he realized that Sienna was also walking directly to the door of his next class. Another bonus!

His physics teacher wasn't into the alphabetical thing, so Jason took a seat by the window. Physics was one of his strong subjects, so the distracting view of the surfers riding the curls wouldn't hurt his grade too badly.

After watching them for a few minutes, Jason couldn't wait to hit the water – even if it was just the pool. Thank God physics was his last class of the day. He'd already put his name on the list for swim team tryouts right after school that evening. The second the bell rang to end class, Jason bolted from his seat and took off toward the pool. He found the locker room – the only one he'd ever been in that didn't smell of sneakers and feet – and suited up.

'I hope you've been practicing over break,' Jason heard someone in the next row of lockers say with a laugh. 'With the electronic plates installed, you're not going to be able to cheat your way into beating me.'

'Bite me,' came the muttered reply.

'You've got electronic timing plates?' Jason asked in surprise. He knew that for Olympic competitions they had timing plates in the starting blocks and contact plates installed underwater. That's because in relays, it was all about tagging. The relay team member wasn't allowed to leave the starting block until he'd been tagged, and the contact plates left no room for error. If a swimmer left the block before his team-mate hit the underwater plate, an alarm was sent to the meet official's headphones and the team would be disqualified. It was pretty hardcore.

This has to be the only high school in the country with an Olympic level system, Jason thought with a grin.

A guy from Jason's calc class, Brad Moreau, appeared around the corner, carrying his goggles. 'We've also got high-speed cameras now,' he told Jason. 'Absolutely nothing is left to human error.' He sat down on one of the polished wooden benches and looped his towel around his neck.

Jason remembered that Adam had put Brad in the DeVere Heights 'rock stars' category, and he could see why. The guy had brown hair and brown eyes – nothing remarkable there – but there was something compelling about him that Jason couldn't quite put his finger on.

'From what I hear, you're going to give us some much-needed aid in the relay,' Brad continued.

Do they give out files on all the new kids, or what?
Jason wondered.

'Small school,' Brad said, reading Jason's expression.
'And Coach Middleton has a big mouth.' He stood up.
'Come on, I'll take you out there.'

'Cool.' Jason grabbed his towel and followed Brad
toward the pool door. He was struck by the fact that
Brad seemed pretty friendly. He'd gotten the
impression from Adam that the DeVere Heights kids
didn't let outsiders in too easily.

But I'm from DeVere Heights, too, he realized
suddenly. Jason was so used to thinking of himself as
ordinary that he'd forgotten his new status as a semi-
wealthy dude. Maybe that was why Brad was acting as
if they were already friends. Was Adam right about
DeVere Heights? Did living behind that gate – a gate,
incidentally, that looked like it should be in a museum
as a piece of sculpture – mean that much to everyone
out here?

'There you have it,' Brad said.

Jason's mouth actually dropped open when he saw
the pool. He estimated it to be fifty meters by ten lanes,
with two moveable bulkheads so that courses could be
set up for twenty-five yards, twenty-five meters or
thirty meters for water polo. It looked like it had a

moveable floor to change the depth, too. And the water was so blue it left an after-image when he blinked.

'Nice, huh?' Brad asked.

'Yeah, sure, but where are the inner tubes? A pool isn't a pool without inner tubes,' Jason joked.

'And a few girls in bikinis,' Brad agreed.

'Get in there and do some warm-up laps,' Coach Middleton called from the bleachers.

Jason was underwater almost before the last word was out of the coach's mouth.

Oh, yeah, I could do this forever, he thought. It was like listening to music to the point where you're gone, not in your head anymore, not exactly anywhere – more like *everywhere.* Jason lost himself in the moment. He could feel nothing but his muscles working, the water pressing against him, the feel of it flowing over his skin. Perfection.

Too soon, the coach blew his whistle and waved everyone over to the side of the pool. 'OK, everybody who's trying out for the team, Assistant Coach Simkins will take you through your paces.' He gestured to a twenty-something guy with a face tanned almost the same color as his freckles.

'Let's head to the other side,' Simkins called, starting around the pool toward the far side.

Jason began to swim over with the other newbies.

'Not you, Freeman. I want you with me,' Coach Middleton said. 'We lost a key man on our two hundred-meter medley team and I need to get you in place asap. From what I hear, you're up to the challenge.'

'Great!' Jason replied. He was up for anything that involved water. And he was starting to get used to the idea that everybody here seemed to know everything about him already.

'Let's try you with Moreau,' he pointed to Brad, 'Van Dyke, and Harberts.'

Jason recognized Van Dyke from English. He didn't think Harberts was in any of his classes.

'I'll take anchor – the freestyle leg,' Van Dyke said.

'You sure you're up to it? You don't look like you're feeling so—' Brad began.

'Don't be trying to nab my spot!' Van Dyke joked. 'You need me as anchor, even though it pains me to have to do the last leg because it means I have to watch you clowns burn up the seconds on your laps – seconds I then have to make up.' Van Dyke turned to Jason. 'I hope you can keep up.'

Jason hoped so too. All three of the guys, but especially Brad and Van Dyke, looked like serious athletes, at least judging by how ripped they were.

Although, Jason could see why Brad was concerned about Van Dyke. His face was pale, death pale, the kind of pale that often precedes a massive puke.

'I'll start us out with the backstroke,' Brad said. 'You can swim breaststroke, Freeman. Then Harberts with fly. Then we'll see if Van Dyke can stay afloat as anchor.'

Jason and Harberts nodded. Somehow it felt natural for Brad to call the line-up. Jason walked over to his block and got into position with his feet at the back. He liked to do a single step to launch himself. He was glad he'd been assigned the breaststroke leg. His freestyle wasn't bad – he'd taken the anchor slot a few times back at his old school – and his butterfly was decent, but his backstroke could use improvement, to put it kindly.

Jason watched as Brad got into the pool at the other end.

'Swimmers, take your mark!' Coach Middleton yelled.

Brad compressed himself into a ball. The coach gave them the signal, and Brad exploded out of the blocks, using his legs to push free. Man, he was fast. Eyes narrowed, Jason watched Brad closely. He couldn't start before Brad touched the plate in the wall, but he didn't want to waste one tenth of a second of his leg of the relay by starting late. He only had fifty meters to show his stuff. Then it would be over to Harberts, who would swim butterfly back to this end where Van Dyke would be waiting to dive in and take the final, freestyle leg.

Brad touched the plate. *Now!* Jason ordered himself. He took a step and flew into the air, then hit the water swimming the breaststroke. *Go through the smallest hole in the water*, Jason coached himself. *Don't pull your arms back. Just scull, scull.*

And then he was done.

Harberts flew over Jason's head and plunged into the water, as Jason climbed out of the pool and watched him swim down to Van Dyke. *These guys are good*, he thought, as Van Dyke made a low, clean entry at the start of his leg.

But then Van Dyke sank! Like his body had turned to lead, that's how fast he went down. Straight to the bottom of the pool.

Jason's lifesaving training kicked in and he raced along the side and plunged back into the pool without even thinking. In a second he had looped one arm around Van Dyke's chest, pulled him to the surface and towed him to the side. Brad and the assistant coach, Simkins, helped hoist him out of the pool.

Van Dyke had been pale before, but Jason saw that even his lips were white now – his gums and his tongue, too.

'Should I get the nurse?' Jason offered. He wasn't sure, but he thought he'd seen the nurse's office somewhere near the principal's.

'Nah. We just need to get him rehydrated,' Brad said confidently. 'And get him some air.' He waved Jason away, then Brad and Simkins led Van Dyke into the locker room, clearly supporting most of his weight.

Harberts jogged over to Jason. 'What the hell was that? Is Van Dyke all right?' he asked.

Jason shrugged. 'He looked completely damaged. But, I don't know . . .' Jason replied doubtfully. He couldn't believe Van Dyke wasn't on a stretcher right now. The inside of his mouth had been as white as his teeth. That wasn't a take-two-aspirin kind of thing.

'Guess he should have listened to Brad and taken it easy,' Harberts said. 'Although easy is not Van Dyke's style.'

'Competitive, huh?' Jason asked, trying to push the image of Van Dyke's limp body out of his mind.

'Extremely, in everything, and mostly with Brad – probably because they usually come in within a second of each other,' Harberts answered. 'And because

Brad ended up with the girl Van Dyke had his eye—'

'Set me up, Harberts!'

Harberts broke off as Van Dyke's voice interrupted.

Jason couldn't believe his eyes. Van Dyke was powering over to his starting block as if nothing had happened.

'Are you sure you know what you're doing?' Simkins called, following Van Dyke out of the locker room. Jason noticed that the assistant coach's face was pale under his tan, each of his freckles now clearly visible. Obviously, he'd been as freaked by Van Dyke's collapse as Jason had. Except that, other than the pale, he didn't actually *seem* wigged out. In fact, Jason thought, he looked more like he'd just snared an admirable buzz.

'Sure, I'm sure,' Van Dyke replied cheerfully.

'Well, *I'm* sure you're hitting the showers,' Coach Middleton yelled. 'I want you in top form for the first meet.'

At least somebody around here is sane, Jason thought. His old coach would definitely have sent Van Dyke to the nurse. Maybe even ordered him to go to the doctor and get blood work done.

'I'm in top form already!' Van Dyke protested, with a grin. And even from where Jason was standing, it was clear that the interior of his mouth was now a healthy deep, dark pink – almost red. His cheeks were flushed too, like he'd been running a marathon.

'I got juiced up,' Van Dyke announced. 'Simkins supplied the sweet, sweet Gatorade.'

Gatorade? Jason shook his head. Clearly they made it differently out here.

After practice, Jason meandered toward his car, enjoying the warmth in his body from the combo of exercise and a hot shower – not to mention the omnipresent sunshine of Malibu. How disturbing would it be to have a seventy-five degree Christmas this winter? Jason smiled to himself; somehow, decorating a palm tree on the beach wouldn't be quite the same as stringing lights on a pine tree.

'Hey, Michigan! Can I borrow your cell? Mine died.'

Jason already knew that voice. Sienna. He felt his pulse quicken as he walked over to her and the imported Alfa Romeo Spider – hood up – that she was leaning on.

'What did you do to your car, Malibu?' he teased.

Sienna shrugged. 'It's temperamental.'

'Oh, well, temperamental, that's beyond me. I could fill up the wiper fluid thing. You out of wiper fluid?' Jason asked.

'Nope,' she answered. 'So I guess you're no help to me.'

'And that's where you're wrong. I know exactly where to get you a cell phone,' Jason said. But he didn't make a move to retrieve it.

'So are you going to? I'll say thank you and everything,' Sienna promised.

'Yeah. But instead of saying thank you, just tell me something about yourself.' *Not bad*, Jason thought. 'It's not right that this whole school seems to have the 411 on me when I don't know anything about anyone.'

Sienna laughed. '"The 411"? I haven't heard that since elementary school.'

Oh. 'What? You have no appreciation for retro?' Jason asked, attempting to recover.

'I'm all about the new,' Sienna breathed, taking a step closer. 'So what do you want to know? I answered your retro question. I'll give you two more.'

Two questions. Jason's brain started to spin. *What did you think of English class? What kind of movies do you like? Did we know each other in a former life?* All moronic. 'I'll think about it while I go get the cell from my car. My sister has it.'

'You drive your sister home?' Sienna asked.

'Yeah.'

'Most guys wouldn't do that.'

'I guess I'm not most guys.'

Sienna smiled that slow smile of hers. 'Good. We need someone different around here. New blood.'

Is she flirting with me? Jason wondered. He felt a huge, goofy grin struggling to break across his face and quickly turned away from her. 'Be right back.'

Dani was waiting for him in the passenger seat, flicking through a glossy. 'Finally,' she said when she spotted him. 'I need to get home and have a nice, private panic attack.'

'It can't have been that bad,' Jason said.

'First day at a new school? First day ever in my life as the new girl?' Dani gave him her patented sarcastic head shake. 'Are you kidding? I've definitely had better days!'

'I need two more minutes,' he told her. 'And I need the cell.'

Dani handed the phone over, sighed, and returned to her magazine.

Jason hesitated. He wanted to come up with something memorable to ask Sienna. Something that would intrigue her, not something like, 'If you could be any kind of animal, what animal would you be?'

Maybe something like, 'When were you the happiest

ever?' Jason thought as he walked back to Sienna. *Or maybe . . . maybe, 'Do you have a boyfriend?'*

Although the answer to that one was pretty clear, because Sienna wasn't leaning against the Alfa Romeo anymore, she was leaning against Brad Moreau. Her arms were wrapped around his neck, his hands were plunged into that amazing black hair of hers. And they were kissing as if they never planned to stop.

THREE

The next day after lunch period, Jason headed straight to the locker room. A bunch of younger guys hung around near the bulletin board just inside the doorway.

'Don't even think about it, bro,' Brad said, clapping Jason on the back.

Jason jumped. He hadn't noticed Brad in the throng of guys. *But what was Brad talking about?* Had he seen Jason flirting with Sienna by her car yesterday? Was he pissed?

'You don't need to check the list. You made the team,' Brad continued, steering Jason away from the group.

Oh. That. OK. Jason's heart rate returned to something around its usual beats per minute. 'Great,' he said.

'So listen, I'm having a party this weekend,' Brad told him as they joined the crowd of students making their way across the sunny courtyard to the next period.

'I put an invite in your swim locker with the info. The whole team will be there.'

'Sounds good,' Jason replied. 'Is it just a guys' night? Team bonding?'

Brad laughed. 'No way. It's a house party – my parents' place on the beach. Bonfire, barbeque, bikini-clad *chiquitas*, absent mother and father, the whole deal.' He slapped hands with Van Dyke, who was waiting outside a classroom. 'Van Dyke will be there. But he shouldn't bring us too low.'

'I tolerate that only because ... Actually, I don't tolerate it,' Van Dyke said, disappearing into the room.

'Best friends since pre-school,' Brad explained. 'See you at practice.'

'Yeah, later.' Jason made his way toward English. English and Sienna. Would it be awkward seeing her? *Screw it*, he told himself. He'd managed to cover his awkwardness yesterday when he had found her and Brad making out. It would be no big commotion seeing her today.

And at Brad's party, he'd make sure he made the acquaintance of a few other DeVere 'chiquitas', as Brad called them. Sienna couldn't be the only female in the place to make his pulse race.

But the moment he stepped into the classroom, his

gaze fell on Sienna. She wasn't even looking at him. She was deep in some conversation on her cell. But Jason suddenly felt intensely alive and aware of her, like she was the only thing in the room that mattered.

She's Brad's girlfriend, Jason thought. *And Brad's a good guy. Like today with the team list and the party invite.* Besides, Jason just wasn't the kind of guy who hit on somebody else's girlfriend.

But none of that seemed to matter when she was so close.

'Hey, Michigan.' Sienna's voice jerked Jason out of his thoughts. He turned toward her, steeling himself to meet her eyes as if she were just a normal girl, who got a normal reaction out of him.

'Hey,' he said, happy to hear that his voice came out steady.

'Did Brad tell you about the party?' she asked.

'Yeah. Sounds cool.'

'And . . . ?' Sienna prompted. When he didn't answer, she turned in her seat to look at him more closely. Jason got an extra jolt when she brought her long, honey-tan legs into sight. 'Are you coming?'

'I don't know,' he said. 'I have to cart my sister to the movies first. Sacred promise. But maybe after.'

Sienna laughed. 'Hold it.' She pointed her cell at

him. 'I need a picture of a guy who would rather spend time with his sister than go to one of Brad's parties.' She hit a button, zapping his image into her phone.

Jason felt a blush creep up his neck – caused by a combo of embarrassment and pornographic thoughts about those legs of hers. At least the blush had started post-photo. 'She's having a hard time here,' he explained. 'Adjusting, I mean. She was like the queen of the school back home.'

'Dani, right?' Sienna asked.

Jason blinked in surprise. These kids really did seem to know everything about him and his family. 'Right.'

'Well, bring her to the party,' Sienna said. '*Pourquoi pas?*'

Jason thought, from the one year of French he'd taken, that that meant 'why not?'

She turned away from him, using both thumbs to click in a text message before class started. He hoped it wasn't about him and what a family-centric, boring little mama's boy he was.

Jason stared at her back. Her silky hair shone in the soft light from the wall sconces. What did it mean that Sienna wanted him to go to the party? It was Brad's party, which meant it was basically her party, too. So maybe she just wanted to be sure they would have a good turnout. *Don't be an idiot,* he told himself. *They're two of the most popular people in school. Everyone will be at their party.*

Sienna threw back her head and laughed at something – probably the return message. She'd completely forgotten Jason was there.

He busied himself pulling *Macbeth* out of his backpack. What did it mean that she wanted him to come to the party? It meant nothing.

'Do you have any idea what this means?' Dani cried. 'Brad Moreau is the hottest guy at DeVere! This party will be *killer.*'

Jason couldn't help smiling.

'Nobody said you were allowed to go, missy,' their mother pointed out from across the new cherry wood dining-room table.

'*Allowed* to go?' Dani repeated. 'Since when do I have to ask permission to go to a party?'

Jason shot his father a look. His dad shrugged. They'd both learned to keep out of arguments between the women in the Freeman family. Mostly because neither Dani nor Mrs Freeman ever paid attention to anyone else when they were arguing with each other.

'We're not in Fraser anymore,' Mrs Freeman said. 'Things are different out here.'

'What are you talking about, Mom?' Dani exploded. 'Aunt Bianca knows all these people, remember? She found us the house here because it's a safe place to live! I'm probably safer here than I was in Fraser.'

'Megan doesn't live in California full-time,' Mrs Freeman argued. 'And she doesn't have children of her own. She doesn't know the kinds of things that go on.'

Dani rolled her eyes. 'Like what? What "things"?'

'I'm not sure,' Mrs Freeman admitted. 'But these kids grow up too fast. Who knows what kind of parties they have?'

Dani sighed, exasperated. 'You've been stealth-watching *The O.C.*, haven't you? Just because "these kids" live in Malibu, doesn't mean they're not normal.'

'So this Brad Moreau's parents will be there?' Mrs Freeman asked. 'And there won't be any drinking?'

Jason took a bite of his mashed potatoes, hiding what he was sure was a guilty expression. He agreed with his mom that the kids out here seemed a little more experienced than his friends back in Michigan. But if his mother thought that Michigan parties were supervised and alcohol-free, she was dreaming.

'Mom.' Dani put on her 'reasonable' voice. 'Even if

there is alcohol there, I won't drink it. I'm not stupid. And besides, you have to let me go. This party is vital.'

'Vital to what?' Mr Freeman asked.

'Vital to making friends. To achieving some kind of happiness at the new school that you're *forcing* me to go to. Isn't that what you want me to do?'

Their parents exchanged a look. Dani's constant misery over the move had been worrying them, Jason knew.

'Look. I ate lunch with Kristy Blane today and yesterday,' Dani said. 'She's really cool. And if I can get her an invitation to a party like this, it will solidify our friendship. Jason, help me out here.'

Jason sighed. The last thing he wanted to do was chaperone Dani and this Kristy person. But this was the first time he'd seen his sister excited about anything since they'd arrived in California. 'Mom, Dani's been going to parties for years. You can't just change the rules because we moved.'

His mom sighed, still unsure.

'Don't worry,' Jason added. 'I'll keep an eye out for her.'

'OK. But be careful,' Mrs Freeman reluctantly agreed. 'I hope I don't regret this.'

I hope I don't regret it, Jason thought.

* * *

'Dani, we're going to be late,' Jason called on Saturday night. He was talking *late* late, not just don't-want-to-look-desperate late. He'd been sitting on the couch for half an hour, waiting for Dani and Kristy to finish getting ready.

'What do you think?' Dani asked as she came down the stairs. She did a turn in front of him. 'Too slutty?'

'Oh, that is so not a question you ask an older brother. An older brother does not even want to *hear* the word "slutty" come out of his sister's mouth,' Jason replied, covering his ears in mock horror. Then he looked at her outfit. It was a tight, short T-shirt and some kind of ruffled miniskirt.

'It's a Stella McCartney. How can it not be perfection?' Kristy demanded from the stairs. She was wearing almost the same outfit in different colors, and her shoulder-length blond hair was styled the same way as Dani's. 'Besides, it's a beach party.'

'Fine, then. It's great. Wear it.' Jason stood up. 'Let's go.'

'No, now you've ruined it for me. I have to change,' Dani said.

'How did I ruin it for you? I didn't even say anything!' Jason protested.

But Dani had disappeared up the stairs, taking Kristy with her.

Jason sank back down with a sigh. Maybe it didn't matter how late they were. He had a feeling that this party would run all night. The way kids at school had been talking about it for the whole week, you'd think Brad's parties were the wildest bashes ever thrown, with people making out on the beach until the sun came up. He was curious to see if the reality lived up to the hype.

He grabbed the remote and clicked on the TV. There was never anything good on on Saturday nights, but he had to distract himself somehow. He couldn't just keep staring at the wall until Dani was finally ready. Why did girls work so hard at their clothes, anyway? Were they all like that? Was Sienna? He wondered if she'd be wearing some little Stella McCartney skirt to the party. He wouldn't mind seeing her in that. Then again, maybe she'd just wear a bathing suit – it was a beach party, after all. Would she wear a bikini and show off those long legs . . . ?

'Dani!' Jason yelled. 'We're leaving. Now!'

'They have valet parking at a high school party?' Jason murmured as a guy in a white jacket waved him to a stop in Brad's car-studded driveway.

43

'Of course,' Kristy said. She shoved open her door and tumbled out of the convertible, followed by Dani. The two of them took off toward the house without a backward glance. Jason gave the valet his keys and looked around. The house was a Spanish-style mansion with a red tile roof. And glass. Lots of glass. Floor to ceiling in some places.

It didn't look much like a beach house. He'd always pictured them as sort of small and rustic. Places you could track sand into, where you could let your bathing suit dry on the porch rail and leave giant towels lying around. But this place oozed elegance.

Remember your mission, Jason told himself as he walked up the granite path. *You are here to meet girls who go to your school. Unattached girls. Converse with them. Share a beverage. That sort of thing.*

'The newbie gets his first look at a hot Malibu party,' a voice said from behind him. Jason glanced over his shoulder to see Adam with his camera. 'Stay right there.' He circled Jason, filming him from all sides.

'I'm beginning to suspect that your movie's about me,' Jason cracked.

'It would be classic,' Adam replied. He turned off the camera and walked with Jason toward the house. 'A stranger arrives in town and shakes up the small, tight-knit community. Very *Footloose*.'

'I don't think I'll be shaking anything up,' Jason said. 'Or dancing like Kevin Bacon.'

'You never know. Maybe you'll end up being the hero of DeVere Heights,' Adam joked.

Jason stepped through the open door into Brad's house and surveyed the scene. 'I don't know, it looks like a typical party to me. No one in need of heroics.'

Adam sighed. 'Then I'll go to Plan B – find a girl to film. Point a camera at them and you're their new best friend.' He clapped Jason on the back and waded into the crowd of kids at the large bar in the living room. Jason headed for the back door instead. He wanted to see the beach part of the beach house.

The wide French doors led out to a perfectly manicured lawn that surrounded an enormous lagoon-shaped pool with a hot tub at one end. The hot tub overflowed in a waterfall into the main pool, and a couple were making out under the spray. Eight more people were crowded into the steaming hot tub, giggling and kissing. Two girls floated on lounge chairs in the pool while a few guys splashed around in the water beside them.

Jason followed a stone path lit with five-foot-high

tiki torches. The path wound around the pool and through a thicket of fruit trees heavy with flowers. Voices floated on the warm summer air – from people hiding in the darkness under the trees. Probably making out where they could get some privacy, Jason figured. So far he wasn't too impressed. Sure, the house was nice, but the party seemed like any other party he'd ever been to.

Then he stepped out of the little orchard – and gasped. He stood on the edge of a tall bluff. The Pacific Ocean spread out in front of him. The moon hung low in the sky, casting a silver path across the water and right up to Jason's feet.

'You don't get that in Michigan,' he murmured.

A tangy, vanilla scent drifted by on the warm breeze. Jason's heartbeat sped up. *Sienna.* He didn't even have to turn around to know she'd come up the path behind him – he recognized her perfume.

'Welcome to California,' she said. 'Nice view, huh?'

'Yeah.' He kept his eyes on the ocean. He knew *she'd* be a pretty nice view as well. But he wasn't the kind of guy who went after someone else's girlfriend. And not looking at her sure helped him stay that way.

'Have you seen the beach yet?' Sienna asked.

'Uh . . . no. I thought maybe this *was* the beach.'

'Do you see any sand?'

'No,' Jason acknowledged. 'But the water's at least fifty feet below us. I thought maybe the whole "beach house" thing was a euphemism.'

Sienna snorted. 'We don't do euphemisms. Coming up with clever wordplay would take valuable time away from the grooming and shopping that is essential to SoCal life. You've heard how vain and materialistic we are out here, right?' she joked. 'When we say beach house, we mean it. Come on.'

She led the way over to a jumble of rocks on the edge of the cliff. In the middle of a boulder a deep step had been cut. Jason peered over Sienna's shoulder to see a steep stairway plunging down the side of the cliff. In the moonlight, he could make out a stretch of pale sand below.

'Looks dangerous,' he said.

Sienna shot him an amused look. 'Sometimes dangerous is worth it,' she said.

They don't do euphemisms. But do they do double entendres? Jason wondered. Was Sienna trying to tell him something? He shoved the thought out of his head and followed her.

She skipped down the steps as if she'd done it a million times. She probably had, Jason knew. Adam had told him that Sienna and Brad had been together since they were freshmen. She must've spent a lot of time at his place.

When they reached the beach, Sienna slipped out of her sandals and took off across the sand barefoot. Jason pulled off his Tevas and left them in a pile of other shoes at the foot of the steps. He looked around at the soft white sand, and the ocean – black in the darkness, except for where silver moonlight rippled across the surface. It took his breath away.

He turned his attention to a giant bonfire that had been built about twenty feet out from the base of the cliff. He hadn't seen it from the top. He got it now. This was where the real party was. A bunch of kids from school ranged along the beach, some swimming, a few playing Frisbee. But most of them were just sitting in groups and couples around the fire, drinking beer.

'Think fast!' Sienna tossed him a bottle from the row of huge coolers set up away from the heat of the fire. He caught it easily but didn't open it. For one thing, it might explode from being shaken up by her throw. For another, he didn't plan to drink tonight; he had to drive Dani and Kristy home.

'Come meet my best friend, Belle Rémy.' Sienna

tugged him over to a tall girl with short blond hair. Jason's skin tingled where Sienna's fingers touched him. 'Belle, this is the new guy,' Sienna said.

Jason nodded at her. He vaguely recalled Adam saying something about Belle in his rundown of the DeVere High hierarchy. But he'd been too distracted by Sienna to pay much attention.

'You didn't tell me he was an *Absolut* cutie,' Belle purred. She smiled at Jason and a dimple appeared in each cheek.

Now here's a girl who seems friendly, Jason thought. *And she herself is a cutie.* She had hair tousled around her heart-shaped face, and pearly skin that gleamed in the moonlight. Her green eyes were bright with intelligence and playfulness. Jason felt that this was a girl he should want to get to know better. But that electricity – that snap he got from Sienna – it just wasn't there with Belle.

'*Absolut* is a word that you can only use once in a while,' Sienna answered. She flicked her eyes from the top of Jason's head to his bare toes. 'But I guess he's worth it.'

With Sienna, the electricity was never far away. As she gave him her seal of approval, Jason immediately got a rush. *OK, not everything happens instantaneously,* he told himself firmly. *Give Belle, like, five minutes, wouldya?*

He turned to Belle and looked her up and down, in what he hoped was a not-obvious way. She didn't have Sienna's curves, but her body was thin and athletic, and she moved with the grace of a dancer. He noticed a diamond sparkling from a ring in her belly button, and smiled. It was sexy.

'Did that hurt?' he asked, with a nod at Belle's navel.

'God, yes.' Belle ran one finger over her piercing. 'I wish someone had told me that before I got it! Do you like it?'

'Yeah,' he said honestly.

'Good,' Belle murmured. Somehow she'd gotten so close he could practically kiss her.

'Hey! Back off, loser,' a harsh voice interrupted.

Jason turned in surprise. A lean guy with shoulder-length brown hair was glaring at him, his blue eyes boring into Jason's.

'Excuse me?' Jason said.

'You heard me. Back off.' The dude stepped closer – close enough for Jason to smell his extreme beer breath. Then, weirdly, he began to giggle. 'Check it out! I totally freaked the new guy!' He slapped Jason on the back in what was supposed to be a friendly way, but the blow was just a little too hard. 'Relax, man.'

'Who are you?' Jason asked.

'Dominic. Belle's boyfriend,' the guy said, his words slurring a tiny bit. 'Didn't she tell you about me?' He dropped his arm across Belle's shoulders and gave her a drunken kiss.

'Her boyfriend?' Jason couldn't hide the astonishment in his voice. The guy looked way too moody to be with the beautiful, bubbly Belle.

'Yeah.' Dominic looked Jason up and down, his eyes hard even though the smile stayed on his face. 'What's so weird about that?'

'Nothing,' Jason said quickly, trying to cover his surprise. 'I just didn't know.'

'Dom, let's go sit by the fire,' Belle suggested. 'You're wasted.'

'So what?' he demanded. 'It's a party.'

Belle pulled him by the hand. 'Let's just go sit.' She gave Jason a lingering smile as they slowly walked off.

Jason shook his head. 'Let me guess. It's a prerequisite for every girl in the Heights to have a boyfriend?' he asked Sienna.

'Well, DeVere's a small school. And we *are* all seniors,' Sienna pointed out. 'We've had plenty of time to hook up with one another. But you never know what might happen.'

Jason gazed at her thoughtfully. 'I'll keep that in mind.'

'Stay away from Belle, though. Dominic's the jealous type. And you're already on his bad side.'

Jason gaped at her. 'I just met the guy. Why would I be on his bad side?'

'Because you were standing within a hundred yards of his woman,' Sienna said, rolling her eyes. 'Just ignore him.'

'The new boy has clearly hit his stride early. Look at him hanging with the most flammable girl at the party.' Adam appeared in front of them, filming and narrating as usual. 'Unfortunately he's in for a disappointment. The lovely Sienna is as untouchable as she is irresistible,' Adam continued.

'You're going to give me a copy of that tape, right?' Brad asked, coming up behind Adam. He plucked the camcorder from Adam's grasp in one easy movement and turned it on the film junkie. 'Let's take a look behind the camera,' he said, imitating Adam's narrator voice. 'Who is the mysterious voyeur that sneaks into our parties and films our every move?'

'I didn't sneak in,' Adam said. 'I came with Jason. Right?'

Jason blinked in surprise. Adam was crashing? He hadn't known that. Still, the guy was his first California friend. He had to back him up. 'Absolutely.'

Brad turned off the camera and handed it back to Adam. 'I'm just kidding,' he said. 'The police chief's son is always welcome. It'll keep us from getting busted for underage drinking.'

'I'm flattered,' Adam said dryly.

'What the hell are you *thinking*?' a guy shouted. 'I could kill you, loser!'

They all spun toward the bonfire. A bunch of kids were rushing to get away from the commotion, and for a moment Jason couldn't see what was happening. Then the way cleared, leaving Dominic and another guy alone in front of the fire. The guy towered over Dominic. He looked like a football player. This was not going to be pretty.

'I'll kill you,' Dominic shouted drunkenly. 'That's my girlfriend you're mauling.'

Jason shot a look at Belle, who stood off to one side. She didn't seem particularly bothered by the scene. But Dominic was almost apoplectic. He shoved the big guy in the chest.

'Hey, man, she asked me if I wanted to do a body shot,' the guy snapped. 'Why don't you yell at *her*?'

Dominic didn't answer. He just charged at the bigger guy, ramming his head into the guy's stomach. Jason expected him to bounce right off the shelf of muscle, but instead the big guy went down, crumpling to the sand as if he'd been stabbed in the gut.

Dominic fell on top of him and began beating on the guy, punching him with both fists, moving faster than Jason would've thought possible. The mountain of flesh groaned and tried to push him off, but Dominic didn't budge.

Jason shook his head. The guy was twice as big as Dominic, but Dominic was going to beat him unconscious. Or worse. Jason was running across the sand before he'd even made a conscious decision. He hit Dominic from the side, using his own momentum to bear the other guy to the ground. They both fell hard, but Dominic didn't seem to feel it. He had squirmed out from beneath Jason in a second.

He turned and straddled Jason's chest, eyes burning with rage. Lightning-fast, his hand shot out and grabbed Jason's neck, squeezing with unbelievable strength.

Get him off you! a voice screamed in Jason's head. He

forced his mind to remember the ju-jitsu training he'd had as a kid back in Michigan. Jason knew that just because an opponent was stronger didn't mean you couldn't beat him. He simply had to out-think Dominic. He concentrated on his own movements, forcing himself to ignore the crushing pain in his windpipe. Then he reached up and stabbed his thumbs into pressure points on either side of Dominic's neck, just above his collarbones.

Dominic's body went slack. Only for an instant, but it was enough. Jason scrambled away and got to his feet, turning back to face his opponent. Amazingly, Dominic was on his feet already. He glared at Jason, his blue eyes crazed. *He's going to charge me*, Jason realized. Luckily, all the old ju-jitsu training came flooding back, and Jason dropped into a fighting stance, ready for Dominic's attack.

But just then, Brad grabbed Dominic in a headlock. He gave Jason a grim smile. 'I'll take it from here.'

Jason nodded, and stumbled away from the fight. But he could feel Dominic's eyes on him. Filled with hate.

FOUR

'Are you all right?' Sienna asked as she and Belle rushed over to Jason.

'Yeah,' Jason answered. The word clawed its way out of his damaged throat. He felt as if he'd swallowed a mouthful of sand.

'Well, you shouldn't be!' Sienna snapped. 'Are you crazy, going after Dominic? You're lucky you're not dead.'

'He's not *that* strong,' Jason muttered. But the truth was, Dominic was a lot stronger than he looked. Jason was usually a pretty good judge of his opposition, but Dominic's strength had taken him completely by surprise.

Jason's eyes moved back to the fight. Brad had Dominic pinned, and Dominic had stopped struggling. Their faces were only about an inch apart as Brad talked Dominic down. The situation had clearly shifted from red alert to yellow.

'Give the boy a break,' Belle told Sienna. She turned to Jason. 'I think you were seriously brave.'

Jason didn't answer. He wasn't really in the mood to be praised by the girl whose boyfriend had just tried to strangle him.

'He wouldn't have had to be brave at all if you didn't love seeing Dominic pull his jealousy act,' Sienna sighed. 'You knew what would happen when you asked Sam to do a body shot.'

'Oh, please,' Belle said, waving off the criticism.

Sam was the huge football player, Jason decided. His thoughts came slowly, as if his brain had been scrambled with a fork. He'd been in fights before, but Dominic had really done a number on him. He sucked in a deep breath of the chilly night air. It still surprised him how fast the temperature in Malibu dropped at night. Part of being so close to the ocean. He glanced over at the water. It was utterly dark now. Some clouds had drifted across the moon, deleting the sparkles of silver light on the waves.

Suddenly, the ocean didn't seem beautiful anymore. The inky water looked . . . ominous. Like it was hiding secrets. Jason had the urge to go check on Dani, make sure she was OK. 'I'm going to head up to the house. See if I can find any fights to get into up there,' he told

Sienna and Belle. Belle laughed, but Sienna didn't look amused.

'You've had your share of fighting for one night,' she answered, her dark eyes stormy.

Sienna was scared for me, Jason realized. He didn't know how to respond to that, especially because her boyfriend had just saved his butt. So he didn't say anything at all, just turned and headed over to the stairs in the cliffside.

The trip back up to the house felt like it took forever. He was really feeling the effects of the fight. He wanted a beer – or three – to take the edge off the pain radiating through several key body parts, and there was a cooler full of them right inside the door. But being the designated driver for the night, he decided he'd have to stick to something non-alcoholic.

Jason managed to find a can of Mountain Dew stuck in among the Hansen's kiwi and strawberry diet soda in the fridge. Hansen's seemed to be right up there with Borba as the non-alcoholic drink to drink, but he didn't plan on tormenting his throat or his belly with something kiwi-flavored.

The sound of girls shrieking, guys bellowing and then both laughing led him to the living room. Harberts and a couple of other guys were playing

Madden NFL on the X-box. Dani's friend Kristy was cheering them on, along with a couple of other girls who looked like freshmen. No Danielle in the mix. Jason wasn't crazy about the fact that she'd split from her friend. He figured it would have been harder for her to get into trouble if she'd stayed with the herd.

On the sofa – a shiny-slick, half-moon shaped burgundy sofa – a few couples were half undressed and making out. Neither of the girls was Dani, which was good. Jason wasn't up for a second fight tonight.

Behind the sofa, a bikini-clad girl was stretched out on the floor, ingesting some vile-looking blue liquid through a funnel held by a guy who had the words 'Slum Lord' written on his naked chest in Magic Marker. Jason didn't think anybody should funnel anything that looked like it should be served with a little umbrella and some plastic seahorses. He was glad to note that Dani wasn't there either.

He popped the top of the Mountain Dew and took a swig as he headed into the kitchen. The carbonation bubbles felt like bombs against the inside of his throat. It was as if Dominic's fingernails had actually broken the skin and gouged out a layer of flesh.

Just like it would be back in Michigan, the kitchen was another party hot spot. A guy who looked as if he played actual – as opposed to virtual – football was doing push-ups with two girls sitting on his back. Another girl was counting the push-ups. A couple of guys had co-opted the granite top of the kitchen island and were mixing up a batch of brownies, with much controversy over exactly what went into them. And in the far corner of the kitchen, Jason's friend Adam was talking to a girl from their history class, Carrie Smith.

Nice, Jason thought. Carrie was a surfer girl. He'd spotted her with her board driving home one day. She kept her dark brown hair short, and she had pointy Jack Nicholson eyebrows – the girl version – which made her look kind of devilish, in a cute way. Jason thought Danielle would give the two of them her potential couple stamp of approval – if she was anywhere in sight. But she wasn't.

From the way Adam was leaning in, and the way Carrie was smiling, Jason figured he might be interrupting something, so he didn't head over. Besides, he wanted to find his sister. He told himself he was worrying about nothing. Danielle had been to lots of parties without Jason playing chaperone. In fact, she was more of a party-animal than he was. But that feeling of darkness that he'd gotten down on the beach hadn't let up. It was probably just a side-effect of getting half-asphyxiated by crazy Dominic, but still . . .

Where was she? Jason exited the kitchen and passed by a spiral staircase. He didn't even want to think about Dani being up in the bedroom territory. Instead, he veered through the first open door he came to – and there she was, playing pool with Michael Van Dyke. Well, at that precise moment, she was actually perched on the edge of the table, flirting for all she was worth, but it came to the same thing.

Jason smiled. Dani had always been a hustler when it came to pool. She looked like a giggly girl who didn't know how to hold a cue. But she played like a pro – she'd been learning from their dad since she was five.

Dani hadn't noticed Jason's arrival. Van Dyke, however, had.

'Freeman!' he bellowed in greeting. 'Your sister is kicking my ass!'

'Well, you shouldn't have told me girls can't play,' Dani retorted. 'You deserve what you get.'

'Harsh.' Van Dyke said, shaking his head and grinning.

Dani bumped him out of the way with her hip, then leaned over to line up her next shot. As she did, she glanced up at Jason.

He raised his eyebrows questioningly.

Dani laughed and answered his unspoken question. 'I'm fine. I'm not drunk, and I can handle your friend here.'

'Yeah, no kidding,' Van Dyke mumbled.

Jason grinned. 'OK then. Later.' He kinda wished Dani was hanging out with a guy her own age. But Van Dyke had been friends with Brad for years, and that made Jason think he was probably a decent guy. Besides, Danielle was clearly having fun, getting evidence that her life in DeVere Heights didn't have to suck, and that was all good.

Back downstairs, Jason grabbed another Mountain Dew and headed out to the pool. Couples were making out at the edge, but he could still swim down the middle. He'd worn bathing shorts in case there was swimming. It *was* a beach party, after all, and they didn't do euphemisms! Sienna's teasing voice came back into his mind, and Jason smiled at the thought of her.

Jason peeled off his T-shirt and got ready to dive into the pool.

'Oh, come on, that part's no fun,' a girl called.

'Yeah, come over here,' another added.

Jason glanced over his shoulder and saw two bikini-clad girls, one blond, the other Asian with glossy black hair, leaning on the little wall that separated the hot tub from the pool. Water from the hot tub flowed over the wall into the pool like a waterfall, making the girls' long hair swirl about them as if they were mermaids.

'Sorry?' Jason asked.

'The pool. It's boring. The jacuzzi is much more interesting,' the blond girl called.

Jason walked over to her. 'Why is that?' he asked.

'Because there are bubbles,' the Asian mermaid replied. 'And steam. And all sorts of things a regular pool doesn't have.'

'Like me,' the blond mermaid added.

'Hey, no trying to hog the new guy!' her friend protested.

Jason grinned. They were both cute, they were both flirting with him, and it was about time the party offered him something to think about besides Sienna. 'OK, you've convinced me,' he said, and eased himself into the hot tub to sit between the two girls. 'I'm Jason.'

'We know,' the blond one told him. 'I'm Cindy, and this is Jin.'

The Asian girl smiled.

'How is it possible that every single person in school knows my name?' Jason asked.

'You're a celebrity,' Jin replied. 'We don't get new boys around here very often.'

'Plus, you're a cute new boy,' Cindy added. 'We *really* don't get those! You were seen moving in and the texts and calls started immediately.'

Jason laughed. 'On behalf of Luke Archer, former new boy, I'm offended.'

Jin wrinkled her nose. 'Oh, Luke. He's such a loner. He's no fun. At least you hold a conversation. I'm not even sure Luke knows how to talk.'

'Well talking is just one of my many talents,' Jason answered with a laugh. 'So, are you two seniors? Wait, you can't be. All the senior girls are off the market,' he said, thinking of Sienna, even though hanging with Cindy and Jin was supposed to be blocking the Sienna thoughts.

'We're lowly juniors,' Cindy told him.

Two more Mountain Dews, a couple of dances with Cindy and Jin – caught on film by a grinning Adam – and four slices of pizza later, Jason felt like it was time to head home. He figured their mom was going to be awake worrying until she knew he and Dani were back safe, and he was pretty much done with the party, anyway. He pushed himself to his feet and headed for the pool room to see if Dani was still there.

'Are you the one who's been hogging all the Dew?' a familiar voice called as he passed the coolers near the front door.

'Does four qualify me?' he asked Sienna.

'That makes you an *Absolut* piggy,' she answered with a smile, but her voice lacked its usual animation and Jason noticed that her face was pale.

Jason gave the soda can in his hand a test shake. 'I'd say there's a good third left. With maybe only five per cent of that being backwash. Want it?'

'Ewww! But even if it was fifteen per cent saliva, I'd have to say yes,' Sienna answered. She took the can and drained it in one long swallow. 'Ahhhh. That should keep me going a little longer. True, Pepsi One has more caffeine, but what's caffeine without sugar?'

'Uh, I'm trying to come up with something clever here, but failing,' Jason told her. 'Milk without the chocolate? Vodka without the tonic?'

'Better stop now before you hurt yourself.' Sienna's smile took the sting out of her words. 'Did Dani have fun tonight?'

'Looked like fun was being had last time I saw her,' Jason answered. 'She was—'

He broke off as Brad rushed through the open back door. 'Somebody puked in the hot tub. I've gotta see if the pool guy will come out tonight to drain and refill. My mom will have a convulsion if she doesn't get her morning soak. Something about pores and heat and toxins. Honestly, I don't listen.'

'So I guess this means you won't be able to take me home anytime soon,' Sienna said. 'I'm wiped.'

'Are you sure it's not dehydration?' Brad asked. 'Want me to find you something to drink?'

Sienna shook her head. 'I just want to crash.'

'I can take you home,' Jason offered. 'I was about to head out anyway.'

Sienna nodded gratefully.

'Great, thanks,' Brad said, rushing off again.

'I'll go get Dani and her friend and we're out of here,' Jason told Sienna. For a second he allowed himself to think about what it would be like if his sister and Kristy weren't at the party. If he'd been handed this chance when he could have been alone with Sienna. There was something about being with a girl in a car – it was like the two of you were in your own private world.

Which is why you should be glad to have Dani and Kristy along, Jason told himself. *You definitely need chaperones. And what about that plan of yours – to meet other girls? Huh? What happened to that?* He had to admit he hadn't been all that aggressive about his other-fish-in-the-sea fishing. He hadn't even asked for phone numbers from Jin or Cindy. Neither mermaid had been nearly as intriguing as Sienna. Which is why chaperones equaled good and safe. He might attempt something brainless, disloyal and all things bad without someone to watch him.

Jason headed for the pool room, but a familiar giggle stopped him in his tracks. Dani was in the living room, on the big burgundy sofa. He could hear her laughing, but the back of the sofa was too high for him to see her. A brief stab of worry went through him; was she drunk? Was she with a guy? Van Dyke? He stepped around the couch and stopped in surprise. His sister was practically convulsed with laughter, all trace of the pouty, self-pitying Dani gone. Kristy sat next to her, also laughing her butt off.

'What's so funny?' he asked, going over to them.

Danielle took one look at his face and laughed even harder. She looked a little pale, and her gray eyes were kind of spacey. 'I don't know,' she answered, her giggles finally subsiding slightly. 'I'm just happy.'

'Oh.' Jason wasn't sure what to say to that. He settled for, 'So you had a good time?'

Kristy snorted, which got Dani laughing again. Kristy joined in.

'O-K,' Jason said. 'You two have obviously had enough to drink.'

'I'm not drunk,' Dani protested, slurring her words. 'I only had one beer.'

'Yeah, I'm not drunk. I mean, she's not drunk,' Kristy agreed. She sat back on the couch and gazed at Jason with a huge grin on her face.

'Need some help?' Sienna asked, coming up behind him.

'I've got two drunk girls who say they're not drunk,' Jason told her. 'Any help at all would be appreciated.'

She smiled at him, then reached out her hands toward Dani. 'Up,' she ordered cheerfully. Dani giggled and grabbed her hands. Sienna hauled her to her feet and steered her over to Jason. Then she pulled Kristy up and led her toward the front door, holding onto her arm.

Jason kept hold of Dani, too. Not that she seemed likely to fall over – he just got the feeling she might wander off toward something funny or pretty or shiny, if she got the chance. If he didn't know her better, he'd think she was stoned.

He and Sienna got both girls outside and into the

tiny backseat of the VW. Sienna took the passenger seat, and Jason climbed in beside her. *Eyes on the road,* he told himself as he pulled out of the driveway. The last thing he should be doing was looking at Sienna's long legs stretched out next to him. *Remember, there are other people in the car.*

Except, after he dropped off one of his little chaperones – Kristy – the other one fell into a nothing-will-wake-me sleep in the back seat. Dani was usually a night owl, but she was snoring before Kristy even reached her front door – which left Jason and Sienna unsupervised in the front.

Just keep your hands on the wheel and your mind on the road, Jason instructed himself firmly.

'What's on your mind?' Sienna asked, ruining the plan.

He couldn't exactly tell her the truth. But what was he supposed to say? 'Dominic,' he said, surprising himself.

'Dominic?' Sienna repeated. 'Why?'

'He was really strong,' Jason replied thoughtfully. 'I take martial-arts classes. I've gone a few rounds with a lot of different guys. But Dominic was, like, freakishly strong.'

Sienna leaned her head back against the headrest

and gazed at him with a tired smile. 'Dominic was just drunk,' she assured him. 'Some people get angry when they're drunk.'

Yeah, but they don't usually get stronger, Jason thought.

Sienna sighed and turned to look out of the window.

'You OK?' he asked.

'Mmm,' she murmured. 'Just tired.'

He took the hint. She didn't feel like talking. Which made it a tiny bit easier to concentrate on the road – until he pulled into Sienna's driveway.

Her house wasn't in the Spanish mission style, like a lot of the places in Malibu. It was spare and clean, with no ornamentation, almost like something carved out of one piece of stone. It managed to distract him from Sienna's presence for, precisely, no time at all.

'Thanks for the ride,' she said, putting her hand on the door handle.

'Sure,' Jason replied. Better to say too little than too much.

'And sorry if I was sort of a bitch to you before – down on the beach, after the fight. It's just that seeing you getting mauled by Dominic . . .' Sienna's voice trailed off.

'I know,' Jason said thoughtfully. 'You were scared for me.'

She didn't answer. Instead she leaned toward Jason and kissed him on the mouth.

Then she pulled away and jumped out of the car before he could respond. Jason was left staring after her as she ran up to the house, his whole body tingling from that one electric moment of contact.

Why the hell did she do that? he asked himself.

And why the hell did she have to stop?

FIVE

'Get up, Dani,' Jason called the next morning. He winced as he lifted his hand to knock on her door. Somehow Dominic had managed to bruise his arm as well as his throat during the fight the night before.

No response.

Jason opened the door and stepped into Dani's room, taking in the totally still form huddled beneath the duvet. 'Dani!' he said, more loudly.

He still didn't get a response, so he reverted to his eight-year-old self. He leaned over his sister and flicked her ear with his forefinger. 'Danielle! Now!'

She ignored him, pulling the covers all the way over her head. 'Go away,' she muttered. 'Do not come back until . . . ever!'

'Mom is making pancakes,' he told her. 'You love them. You have to get up and eat them.'

'I'm not hungry,' his sister said. 'I just need to sleep.'

'Fine. But don't come crying to me if Mom and Dad

don't let you go to any more parties any time soon,' Jason declared and turned toward the door, waiting for the reaction.

'What do you mean?' Danielle demanded, sitting up slowly, her eyes worried.

'I mean that not coming downstairs for your favorite breakfast is like wearing a sign that says, "Hello, my name is Dani. I have a hangover and can't be trusted to behave responsibly until I'm at least eighteen", he explained.

'But I hardly even drank last night,' Danielle protested. She looked down at herself and frowned. 'Why am I still wearing these clothes?'

'That is not the question of someone who barely drank,' Jason told her. 'And you're still wearing those clothes because I had to haul you up here and throw you into bed last night. You passed out in the car.'

'Not possible,' Danielle said, yawning.

'And yet true,' Jason answered. 'I hope Van Dyke didn't have anything to do with your beverage intake or I'm going to have to kick his ass.'

'Van Dyke?' Danielle crawled out of bed and gave a cat-like stretch.

'Michael. You know, the guy you were playing pool with. We're on the swim team together.'

'Oh.' Dani frowned, clearly searching her memory without success. 'Yeah. Him. He was, uh, cute.'

Absurd. She obviously had no idea who he was talking about. 'Do you remember *anything* about the party?' Jason asked.

'Damn straight.' A big smile broke across his sister's face. 'I remember it was the best night of my young life!'

'Dani actually said it was the best night of her life!' Jason told Adam as they slid their trays down the cafeteria food line at lunch on Monday. 'And I've been hearing stuff like that from people all morning.'

'People at DeVere do love the parties,' Adam answered. 'And that one was especially wild. Not that I've gone to many of them before. I mean, I go to lots of parties – and not just ones with paper hats and Pin the Tail on the Donkey, either – but I don't get asked to many *soirées* taking place behind The Gates.' He added a salad to his growing collection of food. 'By the way, thanks for, uh, inviting me.'

Jason laughed. 'Thanks for, *uh*, letting me know that I did before you showed up and all.' He grabbed a pomegranate/blueberry juice. He felt the need for some antioxidants before swim practice. The fight at the party had been seriously debilitating. His neck still hurt every time he turned his head. He'd actually worn a roll-neck yesterday – in Malibu! – to hide the bruises from his mom so she wouldn't freak.

'I can see why you, a near decent-party virgin, thought it a ten on the grand scale,' Jason said, grabbing a turkey sandwich. 'But I still don't know why everyone else is acting like it was *Mardi Gras* and the Superbowl all rolled into one.'

'Hey, I got to hang with Carrie Smith. A girl who is hot and actually attainable. Unlike you, who was busy being friends with Sienna and Belle.' Adam led the way over to the cashier. 'Not to mention your lame showing with the two babes you did manage to dance with. No wonder you didn't think the party rocked the casbah. You were basically there as a eunuch.'

'Rocked the casbah?' Jason repeated.

'You have a problem with The Clash? They're on *The Royal Tenenbaums* soundtrack, and nobody knows music like Wes Anderson.' Jason's face must have shown he had no idea what Adam was talking about, because Adam shook his head sadly. 'Wes Anderson, pretty passable director of *The Royal Tenenbaums*,' he explained.

'Never heard of him,' Jason said. 'However, I believe

that The Clash – and I only know this because of the younger-sister factor – was also on the soundtrack for *What a Girl Wants*,' Jason commented.

Adam stumbled backward, a hand on his heart. 'I'm not sure that our budding friendship is going to survive this conversation,' he said, mock-hurt. 'At the very least, I'm taking you to the Blockbuster in the mall right after school. It's no Mondo Video A-Go-Go – the best video store in LA, by the way, and a true videophile's paradise – but with your level of ignorance, it'll do. We'll start with a few Wes creations, then move on to David Fincher.'

'Sounds cool,' Jason said. He was always up for watching new movies, not that he had the slightest idea who their directors were – and not that he cared. Adam headed over to the usual table. Luke Archer had already staked out his regular seat and was barricaded behind a book.

'So let's talk about Carrie. She looked somewhat into you, my friend,' Jason said. 'Clearly you were managing to keep your true self hidden.'

'She was grooving on the unadulterated Adam,' his friend protested. 'She even helped me pro and con the soundtrack picks for my movie. Unlike you, she has an appreciation for the art that is film.'

'Again, I can see why you're giving the party the big two thumbs up – that's the movie-geek term, right? And I can even see why Dani was blown away by it.' Jason took a bite of his sandwich. 'But I was expecting something more. And I'd definitely have thought that your average DeVere High senior would need more than what I saw to label a night "wild".'

'Wait. You didn't find the true party, did you?' Adam leaned in and lowered his voice. 'Dude, you gotta go through the passage behind the bookcase and take the staircase down to the dungeon. That's where the real depravity takes place. The absinthe fountain, the orgy—'

'You're an ass,' Jason muttered.

'But I had you going for a second. Admit it,' Adam said.

'Ass,' Jason repeated, smiling. But he couldn't help feeling that he had missed something at the party. Not a secret room, but something . . .

Jason winced as he passed a long mirror on his way out of the locker room for swim practice after school. His neck was covered with splotches of blue-black. And his arm, where Dominic had grabbed him, had an impressive dark brown bruise over the bicep.

'Christ!' Van Dyke mumbled when Jason headed out to the pool.

'I second that,' Harberts said from his seat in the bleachers. He took a pull on his PowerAde.

Jason thought it was going to take Harberts more than a little carb boost to be in top form for swimming because he looked awful. He had dark circles under his eyes, and his skin was waxy and pale.

Harberts must have found something more entertaining than the X-box at the party, Jason thought. He'd had at least a day and a half to recover. That should have been plenty of time to recoup from most forms of fun. But the guy still looked exhausted, just like Dani had this morning.

Kyle Priesmeyer, one of the divers, dropped down next to Harberts. He was clearly in a similar state. His skin was ashy instead of its usual warm brown, and he kept yawning. Jason thought the guy was half of one of the couples he had seen rolling around on the Moreaus' sofa. 'Can I have a drink?' Kyle asked, nodding toward Harberts' PowerAde.

'Sorry, man. I need it more,' Harberts replied and drained the bottle.

Kyle rubbed his shaved head with his fingers. 'I can't wake up today. And I slept half of yesterday!'

'I think I'm going to have to start kicking off my parties on Friday afternoons,' Brad called as he headed over to the group. 'You ladies clearly need a little more convalescence time.'

'Ha ha,' Harberts muttered. Kyle yawned again.

'You probably need some convalescing yourself after that . . .' Jason let his words trail off. He'd expected to see at least a few bruises on Brad from the fight. Dominic had gotten in some solid hits before Brad subdued him. But Brad looked more like a swimmer on one of those WB shows Dani watched than like an actual human being. There wasn't a bruise or a scratch on him. He stood in front of the bleachers, bouncing up and down on the balls of his feet. Clearly he didn't need a PowerAde.

'What are you guys waiting for, an evite?' the coach yelled as he strode out of the locker room. 'Pool. Laps. You don't need me to be telling you this.'

Jason was in the pool three seconds later. The coolness and buoyancy of the water soothed his body aches. Thank God Monday practice was mostly just laps of all the different strokes – he didn't feel up to much hardcore relay action today. And, judging from how slow Harberts' laps were, neither did he.

But with each different stroke, Jason loosened up

different muscles, and by the time Coach Middleton brought them over to do a couple of relays, he felt at least marginally human again. He got himself in position opposite Brad. The coach had kept him in the Moreau, Harberts, Van Dyke line up.

Brad hurled himself away from the block with his usual blast of speed. If he was feeling any pain, Jason couldn't see it in the smooth motions of his arms and legs. Jason, on the other hand, still felt his muscles protest a little with every movement. But he refused to let the fact that he'd had a little fight slow him down. *One punch-up shouldn't make me this sore*, he thought, forcing himself to scull swiftly through the water. He punched the sensor in the wall hard when he reached it and saw that he'd managed a fairly decent time.

He could tell from the splash he heard as he swung himself out of the pool that Harberts had made a sloppy start. He turned to watch Van Dyke and saw every muscle in his body tensed as he waited for Harberts to reach him. 'Come on!' he shouted, agitated.

But it was as if Harberts' limbs were weighted with lead. He was trying, but the guy was just too tired to swim as fast as usual. Jason's eyes moved to the huge clock mounted on the far wall and watched the seconds click away. Their time was going to be crap.

When Harberts punched the sensor, Van Dyke threw up his hands in annoyance. 'What's the point of me even getting in the pool?' he yelled at Harberts. 'We're past our slowest time, and I haven't even gotten my ass wet!'

'Sorry, man, I'm just beat,' Harberts replied.

'Dude, he's got after-party. Cut him some slack,' Brad put in, keeping his voice low. Jason figured Brad didn't want the coach to hear.

'Well, maybe we should think about exactly who gets invited to our parties,' Van Dyke shot back. He glared at Brad as if it were all his fault.

'Look, I'll get to sleep early tonight and—' Harberts began.

'I don't want to hear it.' Van Dyke grabbed a towel, wrapped it around his shoulders, and stalked back to the locker room.

'Come on. Let's call it a day,' Brad said. 'We're out of here.'

Jason glanced up at the coach; they still had a few minutes of practice left. But Coach Middleton gave them a nod.

'You had a fish taco from Eddie's yet?' Brad asked Jason as they headed for the locker room.

'I don't even know where Eddie's is,' Jason answered. He wasn't entirely sure what a fish taco was, either. It seemed pretty self-explanatory, but they definitely didn't put fish in tacos in Michigan. It sounded like something to see, if not to actually eat, but he knew that Adam was hanging around so he and Jason could hit Blockbuster after practice. 'Besides, I've got plans today.'

'The sister? Bring her,' Brad said as he dialed the combination into his lock.

'No, Adam Turnball's decided I'm too film-challenged to be allowed to live this close to Hollywood. We're hitting the video store,' Jason explained as he toweled off. 'He might be up for the taco thing instead, though.'

Brad shook his head. 'Nah. I should probably just head home,' he said. 'My mom did not have on a happy face all weekend – and it wasn't just the Botox. She heard about the puke in the hot tub. It wouldn't hurt to put in some good son time.'

Jason nodded. But he had the feeling that if he hadn't mentioned Adam, Mrs Moreau's good son time would have waited. Clearly Adam wasn't in the same social circle as the DeVere Heights crowd. Although, for some reason, Jason himself seemed to be perfectly acceptable. *Guess that's the beauty of living behind the gates of DeVere Heights*, he thought.

'Let's hit Eddie's after the next practice. It'll be better after we've had an actual workout. We'll need the fuel more for muscle repair,' Brad said as he tied his sneakers.

'Sounds like a plan,' Jason answered. They headed out of the locker room and into the bright blue and yellow of a Malibu afternoon. Jason still thought it felt unnatural for the weather to be so predictable. But when it was predictable in a perfect-beach-day way, he figured he could definitely get used to it.

'What's he doing?' Brad asked, coming to an abrupt stop.

Jason followed his gaze across the quad. Adam had his video camera pointed at the giant football player, Sam, from the party. Even at this distance, Jason could see that Sam's lip was puffy, and his black eye could probably be seen from space – more of Dominic's handiwork. 'Adam's shooting something for his work of genius, I guess,' he said.

'But why that guy?' Brad asked, sounding annoyed.

Jason shrugged. 'I haven't quite figured out exactly what Adam's movie is about. I'm not sure even *he* knows.'

Brad's eyes narrowed as he continued to study Adam and Sam. 'You know what? My mom might still be too pissed to stand the sight of me. I think I'll hang with you guys after all.' He raised his voice. 'Hey, Adam! Mind if I join you?'

Adam shut off the camera and slapped hands with Sam. He grabbed his bag and headed over to them. 'Sure. You can help me educate Freeman.'

'You take care of the film stuff. I'm working on his knowledge of fish tacos,' Brad replied. Adam laughed.

Brad flashed him a big grin. 'Besides, I don't know what you're talking about half the time with the movie lingo. You'll have to educate me along with Michigan boy.'

'Always a pleasure to help the film-challenged,' Adam told him happily.

'Let's take my car.' Brad clapped Adam on the back and led him toward a Mercedes convertible. 'You want to drive?'

'Are you kidding me?' Adam asked. 'My vehicle is a used Vespa. Of course I want to drive the Merc.'

Jason followed them, confused. Brad hadn't seemed eager to hang with Adam at all, but now he was acting like they were old friends. What was the deal?

SIX

'Sorry, Danielle. I'm with your mom on this one,' Jason's father said at dinner the next night. 'A yacht, alcohol, and no way to get someone to come pick you up if there's trouble . . .'

'It's a bad idea,' Mrs Freeman finished for him. 'I'm surprised this girl's parents are even allowing her to have a party on their boat.'

'Yacht,' Jason corrected automatically. Nobody in Malibu said 'boat' unless they were talking about a really old, huge car. And Belle's party was definitely taking place on a yacht. He'd heard enough about it at school today to be *Absolut*-ely sure of that, along with the exact length of the yacht and how many separate cabins it had.

'But Jason will be there,' Dani pleaded, eyes darting hopefully from one parent to the other. 'And Belle is completely responsible.'

Jason couldn't agree with his sister on that one. Belle

was flirtatious and as cute as a basketful of kittens. But responsible? Hell, no. Inviting a guy to body-shot her in front of her insanely jealous boyfriend – that was pretty much the anti of responsible.

'When we've gotten to know some of these kids personally—' Jason's mom began.

'Fine. Pick a night. I'll invite them all over for charades and square-dancing and Hi-C fruit punch. Or is that still too racy for you?' Dani demanded sarcastically. She stood up, grabbed her plate, dropped the silverware on top with a clatter and headed into the kitchen.

Jason glanced at his watch. The Dani/Mom-with-a-minor-assist-from-Dad conversation about the party had lasted under three minutes. It wasn't like Dani to give up so easily. But it was only Tuesday night. The party was on Saturday. Jason figured his sister was plotting Round Two even now.

By the time Saturday rolled around, Danielle still hadn't made another play to get herself on the yacht. She didn't even shoot their mom a my-life-is-hell-thanks-to-you look when Jason took off in the VW, leaving her behind. Obviously she had something up her sleeve; Danielle was not the type to allow a parental party ban to ruin her night. Jason just hoped that he wasn't going to have to deal with the fallout.

Not that he was sorry when he found himself standing on the aft deck of the *Moulin Rouge* with no little sister to watch over. He leaned on the rail and took in the sight of Surfrider Beach going golden in the sunset, the sand and the high bluffs behind it practically glowing in the evening light. Surfers riding the waves seemed to be skimming over swells of molten gold, and when Jason turned to look at the sky, his breath caught in his throat; the sun looked huge, a pulsing orange orb that appeared to be sinking directly into the ocean a few miles away. Jason almost expected to see steam when the fiery circle hit the water.

Orangey-pink light glinted off the dark wood decks of the yacht, a 60-foot-long vintage Chris Craft Commander in pristine condition. Jason couldn't even begin to guess how much a ship like this cost, but at the moment he'd be willing to say it was worth every penny. Between the sunset, the cool ocean breeze, and the gleaming chrome and wood of the yacht, he felt as if he'd stepped into some kind of fantasy world.

'Kissabull?' a laughing voice demanded behind him. Jason turned and saw Belle balancing a tray of drinks in one hand. She was barefoot and wore a bikini top with one of those skirts that is basically a piece of cloth and a knot. Plus, the little diamond glittered next to her belly button and silver rings shone on a couple of her toes.

'Kissable?' Jason repeated, because he wasn't sure what to say. Was she asking him if *he* was or telling him that *she* was?

'Wait. No. For you, a Malibull. 'Cause you're new to Malibu. Ever had one?' Belle asked as she selected a pale green drink from the tray and handed it to him.

'This will be my first,' Jason admitted.

'It's Midori, pineapple juice and Red Bull,' Belle told him. 'If you don't like it, the Kissabull has Grape Pucker and the Bullionaire has gin, o.j. and cranberry juice.'

'Almost a sports drink then!' Jason said with a grin, not liking to admit he had no idea what Midori – or Grape Pucker, for that matter – actually was. He took a sip of his drink. It was a weak, sweet girly thing, with only the tiniest bit of a kick. It tasted exactly like something he'd expect Belle to serve. He smiled at her. 'Thanks.'

'I live to serve. But only the first round. Then the crew takes over.' Belle moved on with her tray.

A moment later, Harberts took her place in front of

Jason. He shook his head when he saw the drink in Jason's hand. 'If you're trying to get a little happy-head, I gotta tell you that thing is only a few steps above non-alcoholic beer.' He shook his glass. 'Vodka and tonic. Now *this* is the real deal.'

Jason grabbed Harberts' drink and took a pull.

'Hey!' Harberts protested.

Jason grinned. 'I'm doing you a favor.' He handed Harberts the Malibull. 'You'll thank me at practice on Monday. Don't want a repeat of last week.'

'Aaron, I've been looking for you.' A tall girl in a shortie wetsuit sauntered over to them. 'You said you'd snorkel with me.'

'I thought you meant the kind of snorkeling we did at Brad's party,' Harberts joked.

The girl gave him a playful slap on the arm. 'I'm Maggie, by the way,' she told Jason as she twisted her long golden-brown hair into a bun at the back of her head. 'Since Aaron's too rude to introduce us.'

Harberts rolled his eyes. 'Maggie's on the girls' relay team. A medley swimmer like us,' he said. He ran his hand down the form-fitting neoprene that fit Maggie like a snake's skin.

'I should have known you're a swimmer,' Maggie said. Her hazel eyes meandered over Jason's body.

'You've got the build for it. You want to be my snorkeling buddy if Aaron isn't—?'

'Aaron is,' Harberts interrupted. 'And Jason has plans of his own.'

Jason took the hint and wandered to the other side of the deck. There was plenty of room for wandering on this yacht. He spotted Luke Archer standing by himself, as usual, and staring into the foamy white wake. 'Hey,' Jason greeted him. 'I didn't expect to see the mysterious school loner at a party. I don't think I've ever seen you away from our lunch table.'

Luke's lips twisted into a wry smile. 'Sometimes I like to do the lonely-in-a-crowd variation. Just to mix things up.'

'First time I've seen you without a book in your hands, too,' Jason commented, leaning on the rail next to him.

Luke pulled a novel out of his back pocket. Jason took that as another hint.

'OK. I'll let you get to it,' he said and headed down the stairs and into a lounge with a widescreen TV and a killer sound system. Guster bongoed away out of multiple speakers, and he noticed Adam standing in the entrance to the hallway across the room, filming as always.

Jason finished off his vodka and tonic as he wove through the crowd and over to his friend. He followed the angle of Adam's camera, and found himself looking into one of the cabins. More specifically, at the bed. Even more specifically, at Carrie Smith sprawled on top of some guy, on the bed. Her hands were wrapped in said guy's longish blond hair and her mouth was suctioned onto his.

Uh-oh, Jason thought.

'This is not the movie you want to make,' he told Adam, grabbing him by the back of the shirt and pulling him out of the hall. 'What would Wes Anderson think? Or were there some pornos on his credit list that you forgot to tell me about?'

Adam lowered the camera. 'Scott Challon. *Happy Gilmore* is probably the guy's favorite movie, and she's in there . . .' His voice trailed off and he just stood there, looking crushed.

Jason decided a change of subject – and locale – was necessary. 'I heard there's a hot tub on the foredeck. Let's go check it out.' He nudged Adam back into the lounge. 'And by *it*, I mean the girls in it. Carrie's hot and film-literate, granted, but don't tell me she's the only one for you. There's no such thing,' he said, immediately thinking of Sienna.

'Scott Challon,' Adam said again, shaking his head as if he couldn't believe it.

Jason gently pulled the camera out of Adam's hand and stowed it behind a chair. He snagged a few drinks from a passing waiter in some *faux* version of a naval uniform, handed one to Adam, and held his own up in a toast. 'To moving on and meeting new women,' he said firmly. 'Drink up.'

Adam reluctantly clinked glasses with him, then drained his drink in one long swallow. 'That's disgusting,' he commented, wiping his mouth.

'I'll say,' Jason agreed, finishing his own drink. 'But hopefully it will be effective! Let's go.' He led the way back to the stairs.

Two girls were coming down as they started up. Two girls who looked very much like his sister and Kristy.

'Hi!' Danielle said brightly.

Jason groaned. He'd been hoping he was wrong about Dani's secret plans for the night. 'I knew you were going to pull something like this.' Jason sighed. 'How dumb are Mom and Dad not to guess where you are tonight?'

Dani's eyes sparkled. 'What they don't know won't hurt them.'

'They think she's sleeping over at my place,' Kristy explained.

'*Shhh*,' Dani told Jason, putting a finger to her lips.

'You better watch yourself if you expect me to "*shhh*",' Jason said, nodding toward the two drinks in her hands.

'Don't worry. The rum is for my new friend, Dan, down there. Mine's just pure o.j.' Dani crossed her heart, without sloshing either drink, as she and Kristy slipped past Jason and Adam.

Jason shook his head. 'You know this guy Dan?' he asked Adam, sliding into big brother mode.

'Senior. Basketball player. Hangs with Zach Lafrenière, when Zach deigns to attend school. Hasn't spent time with my father, the Chief of Police, if that's what you're asking,' Adam replied, with a grin.

'No record. I guess that's something.' Jason laughed. He stepped out onto the deck and followed the sounds of laughing and splashing to the hot tub.

He stopped in surprise when he reached it: a huge hot tub, filled with people, drinking, laughing and making out. Well, there was really only one couple making out, but that was the only one that mattered. Brad Moreau was facing Jason. And in his arms was a girl with long black hair and honey-tanned skin, kissing Brad like she was drowning and he was oxygen.

Jason's face flushed and his muscles tensed. He couldn't get in the tub. He couldn't sit two feet away from Brad and Sienna making out. He'd done his best to forget the kiss Sienna had laid on him when he'd driven her home from the last party, and to remember that she and Brad were together. But that didn't mean he wanted a front row seat for their groping.

Brad moved his lips from Sienna's mouth to her shoulder, turning her head a little in the bubbling water, and revealing not Sienna's face, but the face of Lauren Gissinger, a girl in Jason's physics class.

Not Sienna. Relief spun through Jason's body. It wasn't Sienna making out with Brad.

Then he realized exactly what he was seeing. *Not Sienna.* Jason's relief quickly turned to shock, then bewilderment. Brad was cheating on Sienna!

SEVEN

Jason's mind was a jumble of emotions. Confusion – Brad didn't seem like the kind of guy to cheat so openly. Anger – on Sienna's behalf. And frustration on his own – here he was trying so hard to keep away from Sienna because she was Brad's girlfriend, and Brad didn't even care enough to be faithful.

Then Jason told himself that maybe Brad had had a bit too much to drink and maybe, since he was supposed to be a friend, he should go and attempt to save Brad from himself – before Sienna happened upon the spectacle in the hot tub.

Reluctantly he strode over to the hot tub and tapped Brad on the shoulder. 'Hey, Brad. Are you sure you know what you're doing, man? Sienna's definitely at this party somewhere,' he warned.

Brad looked up, startled. 'Er, yeah, it's OK. I know what I'm doing,' he said, in a slightly bemused kind of way.

Jason shrugged. 'Well, it's your funeral,' he said. He figured there wasn't anything more he could do.

Lauren stood up, droplets of water sliding down her body. 'Maybe I should, um, go somewhere else,' she offered. But she looked kind of spaced-out, as if she wasn't really sure what was going on.

Brad gently pulled her down onto his lap. 'You're fine right where you are,' he told her. His eyes met Jason's. 'But *you* might want to go someplace else,' he said pointedly.

Jason nodded, sighed and got up to go.

'And, hey, don't worry, dude!' Brad called after him. A grin broke across his face. 'Sienna's just as bad. It's all cool.' He twisted Lauren's long, dark hair around his hand and used it to pull her face closer to his. Then he turned away from Jason and kissed her.

'Let's go,' Adam said as Jason came back to join him.

Jason nodded briefly, and they turned and walked away. 'Bet you wish you'd had your camera on for that special moment,' he muttered to Adam as they circled round to the aft deck.

'No. Not dramatic enough,' Adam joked as they approached the bar. 'Wait!' he exclaimed suddenly. 'They've got better stuff downstairs. Let's go there instead!' He veered in front of Jason, but it was too late: Jason had already seen.

Sienna and Kyle, the diver from the swim team, were sitting on one of the leather couches near the bar. They were performing a little show of their own. And it was definitely Sienna this time – Jason had a great view of her as she lifted her body to move onto Kyle's lap, pulling him closer. Jason couldn't look away as Kyle slid his hands down over her ass while she traced the shape of his top lip with her finger.

'Jason!' The sound of Adam's voice broke the spell. Jason blinked, then headed directly to the bar. The confusion and frustration he'd felt with Brad had turned to ice in his veins. He didn't know whether to be mad at himself for trying to defend Sienna, or mad at *her* for totally not deserving it.

'I think there's a poker game going on in the master stateroom. We should check it out,' Adam said, talking at warp speed. 'These rich boys need to be relieved of some cash.' He winced. 'Oops, sorry, I keep forgetting you're a rich boy, too. You haven't acquired the vibe. You should work on that. You can start by observing the others of your kind during the game.'

Jason could tell Adam was trying to distract him. He felt bad – after all, the girl Adam was crushing on had been all over some other guy, too. And Jason wasn't even officially crushing on Sienna, so why was he taking it all so badly?

He took a shaky breath, trying to get a hold of his whirling thoughts. 'You go. I'm going to be too busy getting seriously drunk.'

Adam hesitated.

'It's OK. I'll catch up with you later,' Jason told him.

Adam nodded and disappeared down the stairs. 'Vodka and tonic,' Jason told the bartender. With the amount of consumption he intended, he didn't think it would be smart to start mixing his drinks. He'd been such a clown. Brad was clearly right about Sienna. And why wouldn't he be right? He was her *boyfriend*. He should know her.

The bartender handed him the drink and Jason drained it in one long swallow.

'One more,' he said.

The bartender raised an eyebrow, but didn't comment. He was probably well paid to keep quiet about what kids were drinking at parties like this. Jason took the second drink downstairs. He figured he might as well find out if the stuff was truly better down there.

But he didn't have the chance. Erin Henry met him at the bottom of the stairs. 'New boy. You are going to dance with me,' she said, sounding emphatic and slightly drunk. Those were the first words she'd ever said to him. Or wait, maybe she'd once asked to borrow a pen in history.

'Fine,' he told her. He slapped his glass down – after sucking it dry – and let Erin take his hand and tug him over to the little dance floor.

Erin wrapped her arms around him, pushing her body right up against his, but somehow Jason still couldn't keep his mind off Sienna.

'You like the party?' Erin murmured, smiling up at him.

'I guess,' Jason replied. But it was a lie. For him the magical atmosphere of the yacht had become toxic. What was the deal with Sienna and Brad? How could they both cheat on each other so casually?

'You're supposed to actually move your body when you dance,' Erin teased.

Jason jumped, and realized he'd just been standing still, gazing off into space. 'Sorry,' he said quickly. 'I didn't mean to space.'

'A little toasted, new boy?' Erin asked, her green eyes sparkling. She did a little shimmy down his body and back up again.

'A little,' he agreed. *And what's wrong with that?* he

asked himself. After all, it was a party, he didn't have to drive home till the morning, he could just crash somewhere, and everybody else was drunk, too. Why shouldn't he have fun? Sienna and Brad and their relationship was just none of his business.

The music changed to a slower song, and Erin twined her arms around his neck. Jason slid his hands down her back, the sheer summer dress she wore felt silky under his fingers. Feeling bold – and drunk – he moved on down to her butt and squeezed.

He almost expected her to slap him, but she didn't. Instead, she just lifted her eyebrows with a smile and grabbed his butt right back.

Jason was so surprised that he just laughed.

Erin laughed, too, then moved in and began kissing his neck. Jason closed his eyes and enjoyed the sensation. Her lips against his skin sent little tingles up and down his spine. Now she was nibbling on his earlobe like it was chocolate. Did she have a thing for him? Maybe she had some wild crush on him like he had on Sienna. True, she hardly knew him. But then, Jason hardly knew Sienna, either.

I'm not thinking about that right now, he told himself. He kissed Erin's eyelid, her nose, her cheek, until she gave up her lips, her tongue. He gave a half groan as her mouth moved off his mouth and down onto his throat, warm and wet. Jason felt his body go liquid. He couldn't tell where he stopped and Erin started. He felt he could stay in the moment forever and never want anything more.

The song changed again, got faster, but they didn't break apart. They swayed together, ignoring the new tempo for a minute or so. But then Erin's hips began to move faster, and she stepped away a little, her body going with the music. Soon she was dancing again, their entwined hands her only contact with Jason. He felt a little cold without her body pressed against him, but then the beat of the music seemed to seep into him and he found himself dancing. He barely even noticed when Erin let go of his hand. He closed his eyes and let his body move with the pulsing rhythm.

'I'm going to get another drink. You want?' Erin shouted over the loud music.

Jason opened his eyes and saw her already moving away. 'No thanks,' he called back.

She gave him a little wave and boogied off the dance floor. Jason wandered over to the sofa and dropped down onto it. His head was – ha! – it was swimming. He was a swimmer and his head was swimming, even though there wasn't any water! Or maybe there was some water in his head. Not too much, because water on the brain sounded like something bad. But you had to stay hydrated to keep your neuronians firing. Neuronians? Neu-somethings. Jason chuckled. Neuronians sounded like the name of some alien species on *Star Trek*.

Jason closed his eyes and leaned his head back, thinking it over. Although *thinking* wasn't really the word for it. He felt more as if he were floating. The room spun around him, but pleasantly, like a carousel. The music seeped into his muscles and he felt himself relax.

Then the sofa cushions shifted under his body. He cracked open his eyelids. Sienna was sitting next to him. Beautiful Sienna. He smiled at her.

'Nice moves out there on the dance floor,' she commented. She took a sip of her drink. 'You ever considered working with a pole? You'd be a natural and I hear the tips are good.'

Jason took her drink and finished it, then grimaced. 'What was that?'

'O.G.B, Original Gangsta Bull.' She took her empty glass back. 'Bull, gin and o.j..'

'I was drinking vodka,' Jason complained.

'Sorry, I was actually planning on drinking *my* drink

myself,' Sienna teased, like nothing had changed, like she was still . . . Jason couldn't find the word.

The music changed again. Jason could feel it pulsing through him. He laughed.

'What?' Sienna asked.

'I just like this song. It feels good,' he answered.

'Well, good,' Sienna said. Her long hair swayed with the music. He wanted to touch it. He wanted to wrap his hands in it and let the silken strands slide through his fingers. 'Want to dance?' he asked. 'Experience my moves for yourself?'

Sienna smiled. 'Tempting,' she said. 'But I should go see what Brad's up to.'

'He's up to no good. Just like you,' Jason told her, feeling insanely happy. 'I saw you up there with Kyle. Outrageous!'

'Outrageous?' Sienna frowned. 'I'm sorry. Have you ever even said hello to Erin before today?'

'No. But I don't have a boyfriend.' *Wait.* Something was wrong with that sentence. *Oh.* He laughed again. 'I mean *girlfriend.* You're the one with the boyfriend.' He reached out and touched Sienna's face. 'Did you want me to wait for you? I wanted it to be you, but I didn't know if you'd have time to get to everybody. Every body.' Jason chuckled. He was so witty.

Sienna pushed him away and jumped to her feet. Her eyes were cold as she stared down at him. Ice cold. He hadn't known dark eyes could look so cold. Then she turned and stalked away from him.

The music slid out of Jason's body as he realized that he'd just kind of called Sienna a whore. Or, at least, a slut. He had to go after her. Try to explain. He shoved himself to his feet, but all the bones in his legs had gone . . . somewhere. He wobbled, then slid down onto the floor, missing the couch. He'd totally fallen on his butt!

Somebody nearby began laughing at him, and Jason laughed along. The soft vibrations from the yacht's motor tickled him and the music slithered back into his boneless body. Jason couldn't remember ever feeling this way before – so . . . ecstatic!

The yacht was a fantasy world again, and this was the best party ever. Jason just kept laughing as the fantasy world spun around him.

EIGHT

'He lives!' Dani commented when Jason staggered into the living room the next afternoon. 'You should be very happy that Mom and Dad went to go look at wallpaper all day.'

'You lecturing me, Miss . . . Miss Liar?' He sat down, grabbed the box of Cocoa Puffs off the coffee table and shook some into his mouth. 'These things are loud,' he said as he chewed.

'Not so much if you use milk,' Danielle said, taking a bite of cereal. She looked as wasted as he felt. And judging by the cereal on the table at three in the afternoon, she'd slept pretty late herself. 'The *spoon* actually feels heavy,' she complained.

'After last weekend, I thought you'd be smart enough to cut back on the drinks,' Jason commented.

'All I had was o.j.. All night.' Dani yawned. 'Do you think somebody could have slipped me something?'

'Maybe a bartender. At *your* request,' Jason

suggested. 'You didn't really go the whole night with no alcohol?'

'Yeah, I did,' Dani countered. 'And you should be glad I did. Because it meant I was sober enough to drive you home!'

'You don't have a license,' Jason reminded her.

Dani lifted her hands up and down like she was weighing something. 'Sober and unlicensed, or drunk and licensed? Hmm . . .'

She had a point. 'Thanks. I guess,' Jason managed. He ate another mouthful of Cocoa Puffs, then decided the *CRUNCH, CRUNCH* wasn't worth it. 'Great party, huh?'

'The best. I'm wiped, but I feel really blissed out, even without the drinking,' Dani answered, smiling happily.

'Me too. No wonder everyone wants to do the DeVere Heights parties.'

'Who wants to look at the new hall wallpaper we picked out?' their mother called as she and their dad came into the house.

Jason and Dani both groaned.

'You go,' Jason said. 'You owe me for the "*shhh*".'

'Well, *you* owe *me* for the . . .' Dani made a steering motion. But she stood up. 'Coming,' she called.

Jason stretched out on the living-room floor and stared up at the ceiling. The room made a slow rotation. The position felt familiar. An image of Sienna ripped through his mind. Sienna walking away from him. His stomach turned over and a sick feeling flooded his body as another image exploded in his brain: Sienna looking at him coldly. Like she hated him.

Why? Jason couldn't remember. He ran his hands briskly through his hair, trying to think. The sensation brought up another memory: other hands in his hair – gentle fingers sliding though it – and a wet mouth on his throat. Erin. Dancing with Erin. Sliding his hands over her ass.

Jason sat up suddenly, hot bolts of pain stabbing into him. Shards of memory from the night before came flooding back. Kyle running his hands over Sienna's body. And Jason himself calling Sienna a whore! Did that really happen? He climbed slowly to his feet. He had to get some air. He had to figure out what he'd actually done – what he'd done to turn Sienna into an ice queen.

An hour and two bottles of Evian later, Jason was jogging along the top of the bluffs overlooking the ocean. He was so tired that each step felt like swimming through quicksand, but he didn't allow himself to stop. He needed to sweat out the alcohol. How much had he drunk last night? Too much, that's all he knew for sure.

His legs felt like they were made of rubber. Really heavy rubber. But he pushed himself to go faster, fast enough to leave behind the disturbing images of Sienna. And yet they kept pace with him. He saw her walking away with every step, saw her face with every breath. It was miles and miles later before Jason allowed himself to slow down, to rest.

Jason climbed down a pathway from the bluff to the beach. He pulled off his sneakers and walked into the surf up to his calves, letting the cold water of the Pacific ease the strain on his muscles. Running usually invigorated him, but he still couldn't shake his exhaustion from the night before. Slowly, he walked toward home, ignoring the cries of the seagulls and the laughter of beachgoers drifting over the dunes. The sun was low in the sky now, making his shadow stretch out a long way to his left.

As he neared the stretch of beach near Brad's house, Jason spotted the last thing he wanted to see: a group of people from school. More specifically, a group of girls from DeVere Heights, spread out on blankets and beach towels. He'd bet Sienna was one of them. And maybe Erin. Jason slowed down, squinting into the sun to get a better look at who was there. Did he want to see Sienna? Or Erin, for that matter? It would be awkward with either one of them.

He hesitated, wondering if he should climb back up the bluff so he wouldn't have to walk right by them. But then it occurred to him that if he could see them, they could see him. And he didn't want them to see him scurry off like a puppy with his tail between his legs.

So Jason kept walking. His heart began to pound when he got close enough to actually pick Sienna out of the crowd. She and the others had begun packing up picnic stuff, a volleyball net and some surfboards. They were clearly leaving. Maybe she'd just go . . .

But, no, she came heading right toward him. Obviously the potential for awkwardness didn't bother her. Maybe she wanted to yell at him.

Jason sucked in a deep breath and walked over to meet her. 'Hi,' he said.

'Hi.' Her voice was flat and emotionless, giving him nothing. Well, he deserved that.

He glanced at the boards. 'I didn't know you surfed,' he said.

'You don't really know that much about me at all,' Sienna countered.

'True,' Jason acknowledged. He wanted to reach out and touch her, just to break through the barrier he could feel between them. But he knew that would be a bad idea.

'Sienna, come on. We're heading up,' Belle called.

'I'm going to walk home,' Sienna shouted back. 'Stow my stuff for me, OK?'

'No way, carry it yourself,' Belle said, tossing her a towel with a grin. 'Lazy girl!'

Sienna smiled back at her, but the smile never reached her eyes. She was not happy. Without a glance at Jason, Sienna started to walk away. Again.

'Can I walk with you?' Jason asked.

Sienna shrugged. 'If you want,' she replied.

The sun was sinking as they made their way across the velvety sand in silence. Jason suddenly realized they were only about a hundred feet from Sienna's house. He didn't have much time left.

'Look, I'm sorry,' he said softly.

'For what?'

'I said some horrible things last night,' Jason answered. He couldn't remember exactly what he'd said, but he knew he'd hurt her.

'The word I'd use is *outrageous*,' Sienna corrected. She stopped and turned to face him. 'I'd call them *outrageous* things.'

I saw you up there with Kyle. Outrageous! The words sliced into Jason's brain. Suddenly, he could hear himself saying them to Sienna. But the words brought back something else: the memory of Sienna and Kyle together on that couch, Kyle's hands sliding over her curves. Jealousy crashed over Jason, like one of those waves that knock you to the ocean floor.

'I shouldn't have said that,' Jason told Sienna.

'But you meant it. You still feel that way. I can see it on your face,' Sienna accused, her eyes darkening until they were almost black. 'As if you weren't doing exactly the same thing with Erin.'

'Yeah, OK, I was. But at least I wasn't cheating on anyone,' Jason said.

'Right,' Sienna snapped back. 'So when you saw me with Kyle, you were thinking about Brad? How I was treating Brad so badly?' she inquired, wrapping her arms around herself.

'No,' Jason admitted with a sigh. 'No, I wasn't thinking about Brad at all. And what I said ... it was because ...' But he couldn't continue. How could he tell her that he'd said what he had because the sight of another guy's hands on her had made him insane with jealousy? Jason knew that Sienna was right. He really didn't know her. Yeah, she was beautiful. But so was Belle. So was Erin. Malibu was filled with beautiful girls. What made Sienna so different? It was like she could reach into his chest and touch his heart.

'I was an idiot,' he said helplessly.

'Yeah, you were,' Sienna agreed, but she smiled and took a step closer to Jason. 'You wanted some time with me last night. You got time now. Are you finished?'

She was so close he could smell that apple-ocean-vanilla scent of her. 'No,' he murmured. 'No, I'm not finished.' He reached out, wanting to touch her face. But hesitated, his fingers inches away from her, close enough to feel the heat of her skin.

Sienna turned her head slightly, closing the distance between his hand and her cheek.

He was touching her. That was all the invitation Jason needed. He took her face in his hands and kissed her, tasting her, taking her in. Sienna's mouth responded to his, and she ran her hands up his chest to lace them around his neck.

And then . . . Jason forced himself to pull away. They stared at each other for a long moment, before Sienna wordlessly turned toward her house on the cliff above them. Jason watched her for a moment as she climbed the steep stairs cut into the bluff. Then he turned and raced down the beach, his body alive with heat and passion and hope.

He veered toward the water, picking up speed, needing it, needing the motion to channel all the emotion and energy those few minutes with Sienna had created. Fast, faster. His arms pumping, his heart pounding with the rhythm of his feet on the wet sand. Spray from the ocean hit his face as he ran along the shoreline. It cooled his skin, which still burned with the memory of Sienna's touch. Now he was sprinting, running flat out – so fast that there was no chance to stop when he saw it.

Jason's bare foot hit the chilly flesh, and sent him sprawling onto the cold, wet sand. His mind spun, shock filling his body. What had he tripped over? It couldn't have been—

He scrambled up and turned around, praying he'd been wrong about what he'd seen. But the girl's body still lay there. Face down. Her flesh cold and blue.

CPR, Jason ordered himself. *Move, go!*

He dropped to his knees next to the girl and tried to roll her onto her back, but she felt heavy, waterlogged. A wave splashed onto the shore, its undertow pulling her out of his grasp. Jason felt the setting sun hot upon the back of his neck as he reached for her cold arm again.

He waited for the next wave and used the thrust of the water to help him roll her over. Carrie Smith's blank eyes stared up at him.

It was too late for Jason to help her. Too late for anyone.

She was dead.

NINE

Jason climbed out of the police car and headed up his driveway. His mom, his dad and Dani were waiting for him on the front lawn. Mrs Freeman wrapped him in a tight hug and didn't let go. He hugged her back, then pulled away, trying to muster up a reassuring smile for his mother. It didn't work – the concern in her eyes was still there. He had the feeling she was imagining *him* lying there on the sand, with blue lips and fingernails. Cold. Dead.

'Mom, it's OK. I'm OK,' Jason said. His mother slowly nodded and his dad took over, giving Jason the father-patented rib-busting special.

'You're not going to have to hug me too, are you?' he asked Dani when his dad let go.

'No. Don't worry. I'll let you off,' she teased, but her gray eyes were serious.

'When the police called . . .' Mrs Freeman shook her head. 'I knew we were right not to let Dani go to that party. I shouldn't have let you go, either. Where were the parents? That's what I want to know. They just waved from the dock as a bunch of teenagers and enough alcohol to kill a—'

'Mom,' Jason interrupted her, 'just let it go.'

'I can't even imagine how that poor girl's mother is feeling. Did either of you know the girl?' his mother asked.

'A little,' Jason admitted.

'We talked about surfing once,' Dani said. 'She was going to show me the best boards.' Jason suspected that that conversation had taken place at the party, only hours before Carrie died. But he wasn't going to rat out his sister. 'She was only a year older than me,' Dani added, her voice choked with tears.

Now Dani got the parental hug treatment. 'You see why we didn't want you at that party?' Mr Freeman said.

'Yeah,' Dani answered quietly. 'You were right.'

'Well, we were going to fire up the grill and have a barbeque,' Mrs Freeman announced, clapping her hands together. 'We have those steaks.'

Jason was grateful for the change of subject. His own emotions were pretty heavy right now – guilt over not telling his parents that Dani had been on the yacht, horror over the memory of C... a basic queasiness over the rea...dy, and just making out with Erin and obs... he'd been while Carrie was falling overboard...ut Sienna good, Mom,' he said.

'We'll do some ...orn, too,' their mo... salad.'

Dani and Jason stood in silence... their par...s disappeared into the house. 'Thank... for not telling,' sh... said when they were out of sight...

'You think I want to kill ou... mother?' Jason ...ed. Right The joke landed with an almost audible thu... ...e people now it was way too easy to imagine any of... The world he loved being snatched away from hi... suddenly felt dangerous...

Dani just looked at him, her bi... gray eyes serious.

Jason looped his arm over ...er shoulders. 'Let's go inside.'

'Was she ... like, de...iorating?'

The school da... was less than half over and this was the eleventh t...e someone had asked Jason about finding Car...e's body. It was disgusting how morbid people co...ld be. He probably would have gotten twice as man... questions, except that Zach Lafrenière had

chosen today to r...
big topic of con...
washing up de...
For the firs...
a pretty ty...
the sh... bea...
it was abo...
wasn't...

...Va... and that was also a ...st as big as a classmate ...re High struck Jason as being ...how, with the sunshine and the place, it had seemed to him that ...type of sordid gossip. But it obviously wasn't...

Jason slammed his locker shut and turned around. A ... girl with long golden-brown hair stood there look... at him, biting at her lip, eager to hear the details ... what he'd seen. It took a moment for him to realize tha... he was Harbets' friend, Maggie, from the girls' swim te... He'd met her at the party.

Do you want ... hear about the crab that had eaten off part of Carrie's ...ft little finger? he thought. He didn't say the words o... loud. He was afraid Maggie might say yes. 'I didn't rea... look that closely,' he told her.

'You'd have to be completely o... of it to fall off the yacht. I mean, the rails are *rails*,' Maggie said. 'How much do you think she drank?'

'No idea. Gotta go,' he replied, and pretty much race-walked away from her toward the cafeteria, even though the last thing he wanted to do was eat. His stomach had been doing a slow roll every time he'd looked at food since yesterday. He grabbed a smoothie from the juice bar, figuring he could deal with that without puking, and a peanut-butter sandwich that he thought he'd be able to choke down before swim practice.

'Zach, here's somebody you should know. This year's new guy.' Jason didn't have to look to know it was Sienna speaking. Her voice alone made his pulse quicken.

'That's me,' Jason said as he turned around, cafeteria tray in hand. 'Jason Freeman, new guy. Until the next one comes along.'

'Jason's on the swim team with Brad,' Sienna added. She was standing next to a tall guy with short, kinda spiky black hair. This was clearly the famous Zach Lafrenière.

Zach nodded. He didn't say anything. But he seemed to take in everything about Jason with one sweep of his dark brown eyes. His expression wasn't exactly unfriendly, more like ... impenetrable. Jason stared back. He'd been hearing about Zach since day one at DeVere High; the guy's name was on everybody's lips – today, especially. Jason couldn't help feeling curious about him.

The most popular guy in school – here he was at last – and his intensity was almost tangible. The guy seemed to radiate energy and *life*!

'Line. Not moving,' Van Dyke called cheerfully from a couple of people down.

Jason nodded to Zach and Sienna, quickly paid for his food, and then headed to what had become his regular place. He was surprised to see Adam sitting there. He'd been M.I.A. in history this morning, but he clearly hadn't used the free time to shower or comb his hair. His clothes looked like they'd been slept in, while Adam himself looked as if he hadn't slept in days.

Adam stood up before Jason could grab a seat. 'Take a walk with me.'

'OK,' Jason said. They didn't walk far, just over to the edge of the cafeteria terrace.

'You doing all right?' Jason asked as they stared out at the surfers dotting the ocean.

'She's never going to be out there again,' Adam said grimly, and his words were like a punch to Jason's gut. He'd been thinking about Carrie's body pretty much constantly, unable to force the vision of her dead eyes out of his head. But he hadn't gotten as far as thinking about *her*, and the things she'd never do: surf, graduate from high school, turn twenty-one, have any kind of life.

'Did you see anyone doing drugs at the party?' Adam asked.

'What?' Jason tripped over the sudden change of subject. 'No. I wasn't actually looking or anything, but no.'

'Me neither. But that's what the police are thinking. I heard my dad talking about it on the phone with one of the deputies. They don't think she got drunk and took an unplanned dive, they think that she shot up and—' Adam pressed his palms together and made a diving motion.

'Shot up? Why shot up?' Jason asked.

'Needle marks on her arm,' Adam replied. He glanced over his shoulder, then pulled a photo out of the front pocket of his backpack. 'I snagged this from my dad. There were a bunch in the file he brought home. He probably won't miss it.'

Jason lifted an eyebrow.

'What?' Adam asked defensively. 'Don't worry, I'm going to put it back tonight. I just wanted to show it to you.' He handed the photo to Jason. It showed a close up of a girl's arm – Carrie's – with two small red marks, not much bigger than pinpricks, on the smooth pale skin inside her elbow. There was a little bruising around the punctures.

'Needle marks. Hardcore,' Jason commented, running his finger lightly across the picture of the wounds, as if that would tell him something.

'I didn't see anything like this on Carrie when I was with her last week. She didn't seem like she was on anything the night of Belle's party either, even though it *was* a party.' Adam shook his head. 'But what the hell do I know? It's not like we were even friends.'

Not true, Jason thought. Maybe Adam and Carrie hadn't been exactly exclusive. But they had definitely been friends.

'I keep thinking it could be something else,' Adam continued. 'I keep thinking . . . I could be mad here, but I've seen some things. If I'd put it all together faster. If I'd had the balls to actually accept the truth, maybe I could have saved her.'

Jason didn't know what Adam was talking about. But he knew one thing. 'This isn't your fault,' he told his friend.

Adam turned away from the water and faced Jason. 'I want you to look at something with me.'

'Sure. Now?' Jason asked.

'No. The video-editing suite is full of Tarantino wannabes during lunch. But meet me there after school. Oh, but I guess you have practice?'

'I can get out of it if this is important,' Jason told him.

'It is,' Adam said. His eyes glittered and his cheeks were flushed, almost like he had a fever. He turned his face away for a moment, and Jason saw his jaw clench. When he looked back, his expression was grim – and filled with pain. 'That footage I shot at the party?' Adam muttered. 'I think it might prove what really happened to Carrie.'

Jason stepped into the dim video-editing suite after his last class of the day. He spotted Adam at the station in the back corner, hunched close to a monitor. Had Adam really caught something revealing on film? he wondered. Or was this just a reaction to Carrie's death?

'Hey,' he said as he pulled up a chair next to his friend.

Adam's body jerked in surprise. 'Didn't hear you come in,' he muttered.

'Got here as fast as I could,' Jason replied. 'What you got for me?'

'It could be dangerous for you to see,' Adam said, his voice so low Jason almost couldn't make out the words.

'I don't give a crap. Show me,' Jason told him. He was a lot more worried about Adam than about anything he might see on the film. His friend was acting pretty crazy.

Adam brought his hands to the keyboard, then hesitated. 'You know how I've been making this movie . . .'

'Yeah?'

'Well, for a while – since before you got here – it mostly hasn't been a movie. It's been . . . well, research, I guess you'd call it,' Adam went on. 'Because when I was making the movie, I started noticing things . . .' He stared at the monitor. An image of Carrie and Scott Challon was frozen on the screen, Carrie and Scott on the bed in one of the *Moulin Rouge*'s cabins. 'Things somebody like me shouldn't see,' Adam finally added.

'What's that supposed to mean? *Somebody like you*?' Jason asked. He wanted to cover the image of Carrie and Scott with his hands. Adam was in even worse shape than Jason had thought. He didn't need to be looking at that right now.

'There are two groups at DeVere. Everyone knows it,' Adam said. 'I don't know why it took me so long to see exactly what they were . . . I suspected, made lists, took notes and kept filming. But I didn't say anything. I should have told Carrie, warned her.'

'Look, maybe it would be better if you just showed

me what you want to show me,' Jason suggested gently. Once he had facts, maybe he could figure out how to help Adam. Right now he had no idea what was going on in his friend's head.

'OK.' Adam's fingers flew over the keyboard, and a new image appeared on the screen – Brad and Lauren stretched out on one of the lounge chairs on the fore-deck of the yacht. Both dripping with water, clearly just out of the hot tub.

'I saw the coming attractions for this. Didn't make me want to see the movie,' Jason said uneasily. The joke was limp, and he knew it, but he had to say something to hide the wave of humiliation that crashed over him as he remembered what a fool he'd been, scolding Brad like some wrinkled-up prude while Sienna was—

Focus! Jason ordered himself. *This isn't about you.* 'What am I supposed to be seeing?' he asked Adam. Because it couldn't be Brad hovering over the base of Lauren's throat, which is all Jason saw on the monitor. The action was creeping forward, frame by frame, on super slo-mo.

'Wait,' Adam said. 'It's coming up. Right . . . here.' On the screen, Brad raised his head. 'Look at his mouth and her neck,' Adam instructed, hitting a button on the keyboard to freeze the scene.

Jason leaned closer to the monitor. Something dripped from Brad's mouth – something red – and Lauren's throat was smeared with crimson. 'Is that blood?' he asked.

'You see a ketchup bottle anywhere?' Adam replied. He grabbed the police photo of Carrie's arm from a folder on the table and shoved it into Jason's hand. 'You tell me. Don't you think those marks could have been made by teeth instead of a needle?'

Jason suddenly wished he hadn't had that smoothie at lunch. It was trying to come back up. He swallowed hard. 'You . . . you think Brad *bit*—'

Adam didn't let him finish. 'There was blood on his mouth and on Lauren's neck. You saw it.'

'Yeah, but . . .' Jason found all this a bit too bizarre. 'Why would Brad want to bite someone? That's crazy.'

Adam hit a few keys, and the scene replayed itself – Brad at Lauren's throat, Brad glancing up with blood on his lips. 'Look at it,' Adam insisted. 'Just *look*.' He replayed the scene again.

Jason stared at the monitor, leaning in close to make sure he was getting a good look at Brad and Lauren. There was definitely blood – on *her* neck and *his* mouth. 'One more time,' Jason muttered.

Adam replayed it, pausing the image when Brad

faced the camera, Lauren's blood on his mouth. Jason's stomach clenched. Adam was right: Brad had definitely bitten her.

Jason pushed his chair back, wanting some distance between himself and the image on screen. He felt a wave of revulsion toward Brad. 'You've got to show your dad this,' he said quickly. 'Brad's some kind of twisted freak. You think he moved on to Carrie after Lauren? You think *he* killed Carrie after *biting* her? Maybe she freaked and he knocked her out and—'

'No. You're not getting it,' Adam interrupted. He ran his hands through his already-messy hair, leaving it standing straight up. 'I didn't get it either, at first. It's too weird. It's hard to take in.'

'Just tell me,' Jason demanded when Adam paused. He was feeling quite freaked out. There was obviously some messed-up stuff going on here, and every time he thought he knew what it was, Adam shot his theory down. What was the deal?

Adam took a deep breath, his eyes fixed on the picture of Carrie. 'That other group at school I was talking about – the rock stars of DeVere Heights? Brad is one of them. And so is whoever – whatever – killed Carrie.' His gaze shifted so that he was looking Jason straight in the eye. 'They're vampires.'

TEN

Jason laughed. He didn't mean to, but he couldn't stop himself. The horror of finding Carrie's body, the anger of having to describe it over and over to morbidly curious people all day, and now Adam going totally off the deep end. It was all too much. He felt a little hysterical.

'Vampires?' He couldn't even say the word without laughing harder.

'Go ahead. Get it out of your system,' Adam muttered.

'Sorry, sorry, sorry.' Jason managed to get himself under control. 'I agree that Brad is . . . There's something wrong with the guy, definitely. And maybe he did even have something to do with Carrie's death. But he can't be a . . . vampire. I mean, there's no such thing.'

'I spent months telling myself the same thing,' Adam answered. 'If I'd just accepted the truth a little earlier, Carrie might still be alive.' He shut off the monitor. 'So what's it going to take to open your mind?' He stabbed his finger at the police photo of Carrie's arm. 'How about two little puncture marks like these, on Lauren's neck? Because she has them. I guarantee it.'

'I admit that would be pretty damning evidence,' Jason agreed slowly. 'In fact, we should confirm it. If Lauren does have the marks, that will show a connection between Brad and Carrie.' Essential info. Not about vampires, but still essential. 'Any thoughts on where to find Lauren?'

'Yeah. She has – and this isn't all that uncommon among DeVere High students who live *outside* the gates – a job,' Adam answered. 'I'll show you the way. You can follow me.'

'If I can keep up with your superfly Vespa,' Jason said, glad to hear Adam sounding a lot more Adam-like. It was the first time all day that he'd made a rich kid-poor kid joke.

Less than ten minutes later, Jason found himself in front of Under G's, a lingerie store.

'We have to go in there?' he asked dubiously.

'Just remember they only carry European labels,' Adam advised.

'I don't really need a new bra, anyway,' Jason said

and he opened the door and stepped inside, to be greeted with an astounding array of bras and panties and other items he didn't want.

'Can I help you?' asked a frighteningly thin woman with slicked-back hair. She looked the boys up and down and wrinkled her tiny nose as if she smelled something bad.

'Is Lauren around?' Jason asked.

The woman frowned. 'She's not allowed visitors at work.'

Adam slapped Jason on the shoulder. 'This is her cousin from Michigan,' he said firmly. The thin woman looked dubious, but before she could say anything, Lauren bustled over.

'Cousin Jason,' she said, putting on a big fake smile for her boss. 'I thought we were going to meet up after I got off work.'

'Change of plan,' Jason said. His eyes immediately went to Lauren's throat, but a beaded necklace blocked his view.

The boss woman gave the three of them a warning look and moved away.

'You guys are going to get me in trouble,' Lauren whispered. 'What are you even doing here?'

Jason said the first thing that sprang into his mind.

'I just wanted to apologize for being such a idiot at Belle's party this weekend.'

'Oh, OK.' Lauren frowned. 'Honestly, I don't even remember talking to you that night.'

'You didn't. I meant that scene while you were in the hot tub with Brad,' Jason explained.

Lauren smiled. 'That explains it. You don't really expect me to remember anything while I was in the tub with him, do you?'

'You don't remember this guy screaming at you and—' Adam began.

'She said she doesn't remember,' Jason interrupted. He really didn't want to hear a replay of his bad behavior, especially since Lauren didn't even recall it. Maybe she'd had too much to drink. Jason knew *he* had. He'd had to practically squeeze his memories of the party out of his brain. And Dani had been fuzzy too, even though she claimed she hadn't been drinking.

'So I accept your apology. And don't do it again, whatever it was. And please get out of here,' Lauren said in a rush.

Jason shot a look at Adam. How were they going to—?

Adam took action before Jason could finish the thought. 'We're gone. But you gotta tell me where you got that necklace. My mom's birthday is coming up, and she loves stuff with beads.'

Lauren didn't have a chance to answer. Adam slid one finger under the necklace and, a half a second later, beads were bouncing all over the floor. Lauren dropped to the ground, and frantically began trying to gather them up. Jason knelt down next to her as if to help, but he ignored the beads. His attention was firmly focused on Lauren's neck . . .

And there, without a doubt, were two tiny red marks. Marks identical to the ones on Carrie Smith's arm.

Jason scrambled backward, and felt something crack under his foot: a bead. 'Sor—'

'I don't need any more help. Or apologies. Just leave,' Lauren hissed. Jason and Adam bolted out of the door and practically ran over to their vehicles.

'See. You saw them, right? The same marks. The bite,' Adam said.

'I saw the marks,' Jason admitted. 'I'm not sure what made them. But I saw them.' And he knew that meant that there was a connection between Brad and Carrie.

Jason felt like his head might explode. Brad had always seemed like such a decent guy. But it seemed he was sick enough to want to get girls drunk and then bite them – maybe *kill* them! Jason couldn't believe he'd been trying to stay away from Sienna out of loyalty to Brad. Hell, he should be warning her . . .

I should be warning her! Jason thought with a jolt. If Brad was dangerous, then Sienna was probably in danger. And for all he knew, Sienna was with Brad right this very second. He had to get to her.

'Adam, I think you should take this to your dad,' Jason said urgently.

'I can't even get *you* to believe me,' Adam burst out in frustration. 'And my dad's a lot less open-minded than you are. If I say the word "vampire", he's going to have me climbing a mountain at one of those camps for troubled boys!'

'So don't use the V word,' Jason said, pulling his car keys out of his pocket. 'Just show him the tape. And tell him what we saw on Lauren. Show him the link between her and Carrie and Brad.'

'No way. The second there's even a hint of legal trouble involving anyone from DeVere Heights, the celebrity lawyers come out, it gets hushed up and it goes away,' Adam protested. 'I need time to get proof that no one can laugh at.'

'OK. Fair enough. You know this place a lot better than I do,' Jason said. 'But, look, I've got something I have to do right now. We'll talk about this some more another time, right?'

'Fine,' Adam said. 'Where are you going?'

But Jason didn't answer. He didn't have time. He dashed over to the VW and jumped in. The tires squealed as he pulled out of the parking lot. Sienna didn't live far away – nothing was far away in Malibu – but it felt as if it took hours to get up the hill, through the gates, and round to her house. He drove all the way up the driveway, getting as close to the door as he could.

A woman who was clearly Sienna's mom – same dark hair and eyes – opened the front door before he could knock.

'Is Sienna here?' Jason demanded.

Mrs Devereux didn't answer. She just looked Jason up and down as if deciding whether or not to call security.

Jason did a fast back-pedal. 'I'm Jason Freeman. My family and I just moved into the Heights. I'm in a couple of classes with Sienna. Is she here, please?'

'Sienna didn't tell me she was expecting anyone,' Mrs Devereux said slowly.

Jason forced himself to smile. To try to look a little less like a lunatic. 'She isn't. I just thought I'd stop by.

In Michigan, that was OK. I'm still trying to figure out the rules for California.'

Mrs Devereux finally cracked a smile and stepped back, allowing Jason into the house. 'Sienna's out by the pool. Straight through the house and out the glass doors,' she instructed.

'Thanks.' Jason kept himself to a walk as he made his way through the house and out of the French doors. The day was hot, and there was no breeze to cool things down. The water in the pool was perfectly still, reflecting the cloudless sky and the unforgiving sun. Sienna lay on a wooden lounge chair with a plush pillow. Just the sight of her made Jason's heart leap.

Sienna looked surprised to see him. She pushed herself up onto her elbows. 'Jason!'

'Is Brad here?' he asked. The last thing he wanted was for Brad to come walking in on them.

'You came to *my* house to see Brad?' Sienna pulled off her sunglasses and put them on the marble table in front of her. A pitcher of water and a glass sat on the table, bleeding condensation onto the marble.

'No. I came to see you,' Jason said in a rush. 'Is he here?'

Sienna shook her head. 'What's going on? You're hyperventilating. What's the matter?' she asked, her voice warming up with concern. She pointed to the chair next to hers. 'Sit.' Jason sat. 'OK. Now talk.'

'I think Brad killed Carrie Smith. Or that he has something to do with her death, anyway.' The words tumbled out of Jason's mouth so fast that he wasn't even sure what he was saying.

'Whoa!' Sienna held up a hand. 'You've got to slow down. Say that again.'

'Sorry.' He took a deep breath and forced himself to speak more slowly. 'I think Brad may have done something to Carrie. I think he may have killed her.'

Sienna's mouth fell open. She blinked in disbelief, looking a little dazed. 'I have known Brad Moreau my whole life,' she said. 'You're crazy. What would make you say something like that?'

Jason hesitated, trying to figure out how he could make Sienna listen to him. 'Look, I know after, uh, what happened on the beach, this could seem like some pathetic attempt to—'

'To get me away from my boyfriend, so you can have a shot?' Sienna offered.

'Yeah,' Jason said. 'I mean, no. That's what it could seem like. Not what I'm doing. I'm here because I'm worried about you. Carrie had these marks on her arm. Lauren Gissinger has them too – on her throat. And I think I saw Brad put them there. I mean, I know I did. At Belle's party. I saw Brad with blood on his mouth right after he'd been kissing Lauren's neck.'

Jason knew he was talking too much, saying too much at once, but he couldn't stop. 'Well, obviously not kissing, because that wouldn't have made Lauren bleed,' he rattled on. 'Adam thinks Brad bit her, but— I don't know. I don't know what's going on. But I think Brad may be dangerous. You've got to stay away from him.'

Sienna stared at Jason as if he'd been speaking in a language she'd never heard before. 'You *saw* this? You just stood there and—?'

'No,' Jason interrupted. 'I wasn't there. Not right when the biting happened, anyway. I saw it on tape. Adam's been shooting all this footage. He's convinced that Malibu is being taken over by vampires.'

'Vampires?' Sienna repeated. She stood up.

'Yeah. Insanity, I know,' Jason said. 'But something is going on. And you have to promise me you'll stay away from Brad until—'

'Stop,' Sienna ordered. 'Just . . . stop.' Slowly she sank back down onto her lounge chair. Her dark eyes were troubled.

'I know you love Brad, but—'

'Seriously, Jason. Stop talking,' Sienna ordered. She took a shaky breath. 'OK. OK.' Jason thought it sounded more as if she were talking to herself than to him. But then she lifted her eyes to his and stared at him for a moment. 'There's something I have to tell you,' she whispered. 'I'm trusting you here, all right?'

'Of course,' Jason assured her. 'I'd never . . .' The words died in his throat as he noticed Sienna.

She'd been sitting there the whole time, of course, but suddenly he really *saw* her, and his breath caught in his chest.

Sienna's dark hair was glossier than he'd ever seen it, her skin was clear and creamy, almost luminous, and her lips glowed a deep rose red that he didn't think came from lipstick. She was stunning, spectacular, *impossibly* beautiful!

Jason realized he was staring. 'What is it?' he asked. 'Sienna, you can tell me anything.'

And then Sienna smiled, slowly revealing a pair of very white, very sharp, and very real fangs.

ELEVEN

'Adam is right: Brad is a vampire,' Sienna told Jason quietly, her voice shaking a little.

Jason couldn't respond. He felt like he was caught in a particularly weird and vivid dream.

'And so am I,' Sienna continued. 'I'm a vampire too.'

Jason's brain finally managed to get a message to his body, and he stood up so fast he knocked his chair over. He couldn't take his eyes off Sienna's fangs. They were perfectly shaped to make the marks on Carrie and Lauren. He took a step away from her, as his mind reeled in shock.

'Jason.' Sienna reached for him, but he whipped his arm away from her. And suddenly the confusion in his mind vanished to be replaced by fear. Total, overwhelming fear. Sienna was a vampire. A monster. A killer.

And so was Brad.

'Which one of you killed her? Which one of you

killed Carrie Smith?' Jason managed to ask, clamping down on the fear that engulfed his entire body.

'Neither. We didn't. It's not *like* that!' Sienna replied desperately, moving toward him. Jason's muscles tensed. But all she did was set his chair back on its feet. 'It's not like that, Jason. My whole life – the whole time my parents have lived in Malibu – there's never been a death. Not from a vampire.'

'So you're saying you've never bitten anyone?' Jason asked doubtfully.

'No. I have. We all have. We have to feed to stay alive,' Sienna told him.

'You *all* have?' Jason cried. 'You mean there's more than just you and Brad?'

Sienna dropped her head into her hands. 'Oh, God,' she said. 'Yes. It's . . . it's hereditary. There are several of us. But we don't kill people. We only feed because we have no choice.'

'And that's supposed to make me feel better? You haven't actually *killed* anyone, but you drink human blood?' Jason exclaimed.

'Do you think I should allow myself to die instead?' Sienna asked, her eyes bright with emotion. 'It's not like you're thinking, Jason. It's . . . it's pleasurable. It's good for both of us, both sides. It's not even that I haven't *killed* someone to survive. I've never even *hurt* anyone.'

Jason sat down. Mainly because he wasn't sure his legs were going to be able to keep him upright. Sienna returned to her seat next to him. 'How can you say you haven't hurt anyone?' he finally asked. 'Do you get permission? Do the people you . . . you *drink* from, say, "Sure, go ahead, I've got more blood than I need"?'

Sienna swallowed hard. Jason could see the muscles in her throat working. 'You're talking to me like I'm a monster. Like I'm a stranger. Like we've never kissed.' She met his gaze steadily. 'Like you don't know me at all.'

'I don't,' he snapped. 'You told me that yourself, remember? And you were right! I obviously don't know anything about you, because you've been hiding the truth.'

'Well, I'm telling you everything now. I'm trusting you. Not just with *my* secrets, but with the lives of every single person that I care about. And if I'm telling you, I'm also telling Adam Turnball, I guess, so that's even more trust needed. And we're not monsters.' She leaned closer to Jason, and strangely, she was so beautiful, that even knowing what he did, Jason didn't want to draw away.

'Think about it. Think about that film of Adam's that you watched,' Sienna urged. 'Did Lauren look like she was in pain? Did Brad have her overpowered? Did she look like she wanted to get away from him?'

Jason pictured Lauren and Brad on the monitor. The truth was that Lauren had looked like she was having the best damn time of her life. But he wasn't ready to hear more rationalizations. 'Has it happened to me?' he interrupted. 'Has anyone . . . drunk from me?'

She just stared at him, her eyes big and worried.

'I deserve to know,' he told her.

'Yes,' she said softly. 'But it wasn't me.'

He felt a single second of confusion, and then he knew exactly who she was talking about: Erin. Jason remembered the ecstasy he'd felt when he was dancing with her. He hadn't even known her, but he'd been beyond happy while he was making out with her.

'Erin,' Sienna agreed.

'And that's why I couldn't remember much the day after the party!' Jason guessed. 'Because somebody drank from me. Is that part of the whole experience – the victim doesn't remember it?'

'You remembered having a good time,' Sienna pointed out.

A new thought slammed into Jason, making him feel sick. 'So that means my sister, too?' He remembered Dani telling him that she'd had the best time in her young life after Brad's beach party.

Sienna nodded. 'But she's fine. You know that. You can see it.'

The idea of a vampire filling its belly on his little sister's blood nauseated Jason. It couldn't be true. None of this could be true. Maybe he'd been out in the sun too long. And that made him think of something else . . .

'You're out in the sun!' he cried, glancing up at the perfect yellow ball in the cloudless blue sky. 'You can't be a vampire. The sun kills vampires.'

'Watching *Buffy the Vampire Slayer* doesn't mean you know anything about what we are,' Sienna replied. 'The sun doesn't bother us, not anymore.'

'Fine,' Jason said grimly. 'Then what *does* bother you? What kills you?'

Sienna bit her lip. 'You want to kill me?'

'No.' Jason forced himself to dial it back. He was feeling a little crazy. This whole conversation was too surreal. 'No. Of course not. I just meant . . . what else is true about vampires? What's true and what's just made up in the movies?'

'Well, we can change our appearance somewhat,' Sienna said, and gestured to her supernaturally beautiful face. 'This is what I look like naturally. I usually tone it down a little bit on purpose. We all do. We want to blend in with regular people.'

'So you can actually alter your appearance?' Jason asked. 'You can shapeshift?'

'No,' Sienna said quickly. 'Nothing so extreme. We can just . . . modify ourselves to a degree.'

'Modify.' Jason jumped on the small fact, wanting to understand. 'So no morphing into bats or wolves or fog then?'

'No. And no sleeping in coffins. I'm sure that was going to be your next question.' She actually sounded a little hurt. Absurd.

'And crosses, stakes through the heart, garlic?' Jason asked.

Sienna raised one eyebrow. 'I thought you didn't want to kill me.'

He didn't. He *Absolut*-ely didn't want to kill Sienna. But— Well, he wanted to know how to protect himself. Not against her. But against *them*. 'Do any of those things work?' he demanded.

'Well, I think a stake through the heart kills pretty much everyone,' Sienna said. 'But crosses? No. And the only thing garlic does is ruin your social life.' She smiled, and without thinking, Jason smiled back. But he wasn't ready to let the subject drop.

'How old are you? Will you live forever? How long have you been in high school?' he asked, the questions tumbling out more quickly than he'd intended.

'I'm the same age as you,' Sienna replied, laughing. 'And I won't live forever, but most . . . of us . . . do live longer than humans. We age the same way you do until we're adult. After that we age much more slowly.'

'So, how many of you are there? Brad, you, Erin . . . Zach?' he added, suddenly picturing Zach's cold once-over at school the other day. He was clearly the leader of Sienna's group of friends. Chances were good that he'd be a vampire too.

'Jason, I can't—' Sienna began.

'What about Van Dyke?' he rushed on, remembering Van Dyke's miraculous recovery at the first swim practice. He'd gone into the locker room – with Simkins, the assistant coach – and his body had been weak, his gums *white*. He'd emerged just a few minutes later, full of energy and raring to go, while Simkins had come out pale, but looking completely blissed out. Jason suddenly understood how Van Dyke had recovered so quickly – he had fed on Assistant Coach Simkins.

'There are several of us,' Sienna said. 'There are several families in Malibu. But no one will ever hurt you. I promise.'

'Oh, yeah? What about Carrie?' Jason shot back. 'Someone sure hurt her.' He felt anger rising in him again. Carrie was the whole reason he'd come here, and he'd almost forgotten in the midst of all this vampire stuff. 'I found her body. That girl did not enjoy herself with someone from one of these families and go home happy.'

Sienna wrapped her arms around herself, as if she'd suddenly gotten chilled. 'No. She didn't. Poor Carrie.'

'Poor Carrie?' he repeated. 'That's it? She gets murdered by a vampire and that's all you've got to say?'

She grimaced, and he was relieved to see that her teeth had gone back to normal. No fangs. 'There's something called "bloodlust",' Sienna said quietly, seriously. 'It's kind of an addiction – to blood. If a vampire's in the grip of bloodlust, he doesn't stop drinking. He can't.'

'So the human dies,' Jason concluded. 'The vampire keeps drinking until the human is drained of blood.'

'It hasn't happened for decades,' Sienna said. 'It's

forbidden by our families. It's against everything we believe in. You have to trust me on this, Jason. We all have tight control over our urges.'

He gave a short, humorless laugh. 'Obviously not all of you.'

Worry filled Sienna's face. 'Zach is furious about what happened to Carrie,' she said. 'He's going to take care of it. Don't worry. He'll bring down whoever killed her.'

'Zach. Zach will take care of it,' Jason repeated. He pictured the dark-eyed guy he'd met at school. He hadn't looked as if he cared much about anyone on the face of the earth except himself. But Jason had to admit that he *had* looked capable – more than capable – of 'taking care of' things. The guy had given the impression that he was in charge of just about everything that crossed his path. But he was still a vampire. And Jason saw no reason to trust a vampire, especially one he barely even knew. 'And Zach cares why?' he asked.

'We *all* care,' Sienna snapped. 'Because Carrie didn't deserve to die. The same way you would care if some human had murdered her. We care even more because it's one of us and that's unacceptable. And that's why it will be taken care of – by us, by Zach. Because he's the strongest. Believe me, Jason. Whoever killed Carrie won't go unpunished.'

'Sienna, dinner!' Mrs Devereux called, stepping out into the backyard. She glanced at Jason and smiled graciously. 'Would you like to join us, Jason?' she asked.

'No. Thank you.' Jason stood up and tried to smile. But the idea of eating with a family who liked to feed on humans turned his stomach.

'Are you sure? We're having the most delicious risotto,' Mrs Devereux said. 'Our cook is world-class.'

'No,' Jason said abruptly. Usually he was good with parents. But usually those parents weren't also vampires. He couldn't help wondering if Mrs Devereux saw a human like him as part of a herd of cattle? That might be too brutal, Jason decided. Maybe she'd think of him more like a gardener or a pool boy. But would she want one of those types circling Sienna?

'I, uh, my parents will be looking for me,' he added. He tried to force a smile, but his upper lips stuck to his dry gums, and he was afraid it had come out looking more like a sneer.

Sienna walked him to the front door. She touched his arm lightly. 'Hey,' she said quietly. 'You OK with all this?'

He stared into her gorgeous eyes and felt his heart beat faster, the way it always did in her presence. *She's not human*, he told himself. How could he be having these feelings for a vampire? It was wrong. He tried to rein in his body, to stop the automatic attraction he felt for her. But he couldn't. His body didn't care what his brain thought. His body wanted Sienna whether she was a vampire or not. 'No. I'm not OK,' he admitted.

Sienna looked worried, and Jason realized he'd hurt her again. Maybe even more than he had that night on the boat. But she'd asked, and the truth had come out.

'I will be OK, though,' he promised her. That got a tiny smile, but Jason wondered if he was lying. His body seemed to have made a judgment about Sienna. But his brain still wasn't sure that he could trust her.

It was too confusing. He had to get out.

He jogged over to the Bug and peeled out without a backward glance. The sun beat down, bathing the whole of Malibu in a cosmic spotlight. Maybe it was all a dream. Yeah, that made sense. More sense than anything else. A place like DeVere Heights couldn't really exist, Jason thought. It was too extreme. Too dazzling. Too weird. It couldn't be real. Any minute now, he would wake up in Michigan where everything was normal. Where the weather wasn't always sunny.

TWELVE

'I'm sorry, is that a *vegetable* sandwich?' Adam asked at lunch the next day. 'Have you gone so native that you're a vegetarian now?'

Jason peered at the grilled mush in his pitta. 'I'm not in the mood to eat anything that bleeds,' he muttered. He forced himself to meet Adam's gaze. 'I talked to Sienna yesterday.'

Adam swallowed hard. 'And?'

Jason glanced around. He'd purposely led Adam over to a deserted table inside the cafeteria, rather than going out to their usual spot. He couldn't take the chance that their constant tablemate, Luke Archer, might overhear this conversation. Luckily, almost nobody ever ate inside. They had the place to themselves.

'And . . . you're right. She says there are vampires in the Heights. She's one of them. And Brad, like you thought,' Jason said.

'I'm sorry, but ... *what*?' Adam cried. 'Are you telling me that you just went up to Sienna and asked her if she was a vampire?'

'Uh, no. I told her that you thought Brad was a vampire,' Jason said.

'What?' Adam practically shrieked. His pale skin was even paler than usual.

'Well, maybe I didn't say that exactly,' Jason replied quickly. 'I just said that you thought ... that you thought there might be vampires. In DeVere Heights.'

'Oh my God,' Adam said, looking shell-shocked. 'They're going to kick my ass and send me to the loony bin!'

'No, they're not,' Jason assured him. 'I mean, Sienna didn't even seem surprised. She just showed me her fangs and basically said you were right.'

'Oh.' Adam thought about that for a moment. '*Oh.* So I'm right. I'm not crazy. There *are* vampires.'

'Yes,' Jason confirmed.

'Good. Cool. I mean, not good. But, you know, good.' Adam took a deep breath and seemed to calm down a little. 'Sienna and Brad. How many others?'

'A lot of them. For all I know everyone in DeVere Heights is a monster,' Jason spat.

'No way.' Adam shook his head. 'I've known

Bloodlust

Sienna since first grade. Brad, too. They're not monsters.'

'She *told* me she was a vampire,' Jason said. 'She had fangs, for God's sake. Fangs in a human head – that equals monster, right?'

'I've been thinking about that a lot,' Adam answered. 'When I started to piece things together, I kept getting back to a basic truth – Malibu is a spectacular place to live. If vampires were monsters, then it wouldn't be. People would be turning up dead every night, no one would go out after dark, and the real-estate prices would be much, much lower.'

'I can't believe I'm hearing this.' Jason dropped his sandwich back onto his tray. 'You're the one who told me that a vampire *killed* Carrie. If that's not the behavior of a monster, I don't know what is!'

'It is,' Adam agreed. 'So *one* vampire is a monster – not the whole lot.'

'So it'll be like *The Wizard of Oz*? We'll all have to go around asking: "Are you a good vampire or a bad vampire?"'

Adam shrugged. 'You have to understand, man. Everyone who made my list of . . . of vampire suspects, I guess you'd call it, came from a family that is important to this town. Every single charity in Malibu has a Devereux or a Moreau or a Lafrenière on the board,' Adam explained. 'And the DeVere Center – that big brick building up on Cliffside Court? They're doing research into blood replacements, real cutting-edge stuff. Obviously they're trying to find a way to free themselves from having to drink human blood.'

'You're telling me these vampires are out in the open, researching blood, and nobody cares?' Jason had a hard time believing that.

'Nah. They usually do things anonymously,' Adam said. 'But when I started to suspect that they were . . . well, *unusual* . . . I checked into their company holdings and their bank records. I found all kinds of links between the DeVere Heights families and charities, museums, hospitals. Basically – everything that's good in Malibu? Funded by vampires!'

Jason just stared at him.

'I know what you're thinking. Adam Turnball, freak with too much time on his hands,' Adam said. 'But you gotta believe me. I've done my research.'

'But one of these philanthropists killed Carrie!' Jason declared. 'What's the deal? One museum for every corpse? A research institute when the deaths hit triple digits?'

Adam ran a hand through his hair and shook his

head. 'This is the first death I've ever heard of that has a vampire feel to it. I'm just saying . . . they're not all bad. I mean, most of them aren't bad.'

'Tell that to Carrie,' Jason said.

'Please, just stop saying her name, OK?' Adam asked. 'I have nightmares about her. Sometimes even when I'm awake. Those shots I got of Brad and Lauren – they were what totally convinced me my theory was right. If I'd just had the *cojones* to accept the truth a little earlier, I might have saved her.'

'What were you going to do? Rent a van with speakers and blast the news all over town?' Jason said and then cringed as he heard how harsh it sounded. He lowered his voice. 'I just mean, it's not your fault. You didn't kill her. A vampire did. Let's focus on that.'

'OK. Well, whoever killed her isn't like Sienna or Brad,' Adam said. 'The vampire that killed Carrie is evil. Sienna and Brad aren't.'

Jason sighed. 'That's what Sienna said. She thinks whoever did it is some kind of rogue vampire. One that's gone feral. She said it was called bloodlust.'

'Bloodlust?'

'Yeah. It's like an addiction. When a vampire has bloodlust they can't stop drinking. They keep going until they've drained so much blood that the human dies.'

Adam's face went even paler.

'She said it hasn't happened in decades.'

'Well, we can't let it happen again,' Adam replied. 'My dad told me that the cops picked up Scott Challon – you know, the guy who was making out with Carrie at the party?'

Jason nodded.

'Well, lots of people saw them together. I guess they told the cops. And, of course, I even have video footage of it,' Adam said. 'The cops figure Scott might know what happened to Carrie. He might be the last one who saw her alive.'

'So they think he might've killed her,' Jason translated.

'He's the only suspect they have,' Adam answered. 'And I think they're right.'

'So Scott's a vampire?' Jason asked.

'I think so. I've been filming everybody, trying to get proof.' He shook his head and smiled faintly. 'You know, it never occurred to me to just go ask one of them. You're not bad for a novice.'

'Glad I could help,' Jason said wryly. 'So the cops have Scott. Will they charge him?'

'Doubtful,' Adam said. 'And his family is so rich, he'll be sprung in no time. But that doesn't matter. I'm going to find out if he did it. And if he killed Carrie, I'm going to make sure he can never kill again.'

Jason took in the guy's frame. Adam looked like he'd never lifted a weight in his life. But his eyes were deadly serious. 'You're talking about a vampire who's willing to kill,' Jason said gently. 'How are you planning to stop him?'

'I don't know yet,' Adam admitted.

'Look, Sienna said Zach is pretty pissed off about this whole Carrie thing and he's going to take care of it. And *you* said the police are circling Scott,' Jason pointed out. 'Let them handle it.'

'I don't trust Zach and the police aren't going to be able to make anything stick,' Adam said flatly. 'At the moment they think somebody gave Carrie the drugs that killed her. But pretty soon they'll find out that there weren't any drugs in her system and then they'll drop the case. Though I guess they might be kinda confused when they find she's been drained of blood . . . But anyway, we're the only ones who know Carrie's murderer was a vampire.'

Jason frowned. The guy had a point. He eyed Adam, who was drinking Yoohoo through a curly plastic straw. *Drinking it* ironically *through a curly plastic straw*, Jason corrected himself. Adam was a good guy. He was smart, he noticed things, and he knew his way around a camera. Clearly, he'd also picked up a lot about investigating from his dad. But in a fight, he'd be butchered, and Jason couldn't let that happen. He sighed.

'If you're really going to go after this vampire,' Jason said, 'then I'm going with you.'

THIRTEEN

'Heads up!' Adam yelled the next morning. Jason glanced up from his locker to see a piece of paper folded into a triangle flying at him through the air. He caught it right before it hit his eye.

'What's this?'

'The list.' Adam lowered his voice as he came closer. 'I've been working on it for a couple of months, ever since I started to suspect . . .'

'Oh.' It was a list of people Adam thought were vampires, then. Well, Jason knew a few who should definitely be on there. Starting with Sienna.

Sienna. A wisp of her perfume reached his nose. Incredible how he could pick out her scent even in a crowd of people. His body reacted to her, as usual, with a rush of adrenalin. He glanced up as she walked by to see her chatting with Belle as if nothing was wrong. She didn't even look in his direction.

He hadn't spoken to her in the two days since she

told him her secret. He didn't know if he wanted to. Didn't know if she wanted him to, either.

His body ached to go after her, to go talk to her, to hold her in his arms.

But his mind couldn't shake the image of those fangs. Maybe she wasn't evil. But she also wasn't human.

Jason forced himself to turn away. He closed his locker and began walking in the opposite direction. His first class was on the other side of the school. Adam walked with him. Jason unfolded the list and glanced at it as he went. Moreau. Challon. Devereux. Lafrenière. There was a line drawn underneath those four, then the names Henry and Van Dyke.

'Those top four are also the names of the top contributors to every charity and cultural resource in Malibu,' Adam said. 'Sienna's mother just hosted a gala to raise money for the hospital. Brad's father's company just committed to sponsoring a year-round Malibu symphony series on the beach, free to the public, with free barbeque and all. Scott's parents—'

'I get it,' Jason said. 'This list . . . it's a *Who's Who* of the Heights. There isn't anybody who doesn't live behind the gates on here.'

'Hey, it takes a big pile of dough to live forever,' Adam said as he dodged a big guy barreling down the hall. 'If they do. Live forever, I mean. Did you ask Sienna that?'

'Yes and they don't – although they do live longer than humans. She also confirmed that she can't turn into a bat, or a cloud of fog,' Jason added. He glanced down at the list again. 'So this is a Heights thing. No outsiders.'

'You and your family might be the token non-vamps,' Adam agreed. Jason didn't like the idea of being trapped in a small gated area with who knew how many of the walking dead. Walking undead? Everything was a question.

'The families, they created the Heights,' Adam continued as Jason veered over to his classroom door. Adam's first class was three rooms away. 'And lots of those families have French roots – consider the surnames: Devereux, Lafrenière, Moreau, et cetera. The Devereuxs still own vineyards in France and in the Napa Valley. They're one of the oldest families in this area – where do you think DeVere Heights gets its name? The Devereuxs and the Lafrenières have been here the longest – over a hundred years – but it's been almost as long for the other families. And in

California time, that's forever. Pretty much nothing in L.A. is over fifty years old.'

'Is everyone on this list a confirmed V?' Jason asked, pausing outside the classroom.

'Well I was pretty sure Brad was when I saw that blood on his mouth. Sienna outed herself and confirmed him,' Adam said, 'as well as Erin Henry and Michael Van Dyke – or, at least, she didn't say no when you brought them up. I don't have proof about Scott, but—'

'But he was all over Carrie and she got bitten,' Jason finished for him, leaving out the dead part; it wasn't like either of them was going to forget that. 'What about Dominic, that guy I had the run in with at Brad's party?'

'You mean the Dominic who would have beat you into the ground if Brad hadn't come to the rescue?' Adam countered.

'Please. I was holding my own.'

'True. You lasted a lot longer than Sam,' Adam agreed. 'I'm just busting on you.'

'But that was a weird situation,' Jason said. 'Is superstrength a vampire thing? Because there is no way that kind of power should have been coming out of Dominic's runt body.'

'You've got a point. Although *runt* might be exaggerating a tad,' Adam said. 'His dad's a partner in a high-powered law firm and his mother's on the school board of governors. I guess he goes on the list.'

'Maybe that's why Sienna was so freaked that I tried to take Dominic down,' Jason said, suddenly seeing the fight in a whole new light. 'She knows he's a vampire and she was terrified he'd kill me.'

''Cause it would have ended the party early,' Adam said. 'If we add Dominic to the list, does that mean we automatically add Belle?'

'Can you be the best friend of one vampire *and* the girlfriend of another and not be dentally-enhanced yourself?' Jason asked. 'Do they let humans that far into their circle?' *Would Sienna ever let someone like me in that far?* he couldn't help adding to himself.

'Doubtful.' Adam took the list away from Jason and started adding names, including Belle's. 'And besides, Belle's surname is Rémy – that's very French.' He hesitated, looking up at Jason. 'Do you think there are girl-on-girl kind of vamps? I mean, should we consider that Carrie could have been killed by Belle or Erin or someone of the female persuasion?'

'You think lesbianism might be too out there for *vampires*?' Jason shot back.

'Point, got one, you have,' Adam answered. He narrowed his eyes at Jason. 'You have seen a *Star Wars* movie, I assume.'

'A what?' Jason asked blankly.

Adam's face paled and his eyes went wide.

'I'm from Michigan, Turnball. Not the Amish country. Of course I've seen *Star Wars*.' Jason laughed.

'Well, I don't know,' Adam protested. 'Who knows what kind of deprivation you've suffered, living in the middle of the country all your life? Michigan *is* in the middle, right?'

Jason rolled his eyes. 'Let's get back to the list,' he said. 'What do you think of Maggie? I don't know her last name. She's on the girls' swim team.'

'Maggie Roy? Huh. Well, she's from the Heights, but that's the only thing I'd call suspect about Maggie,' Adam answered.

'I'm pretty sure she's been feeding on Aaron Harberts,' Jason told him. 'Somebody definitely had a taste of him at Brad's party – he was still tired at swimming practice a day and a half later. And I know he and Maggie got friendly at that party. I heard them talking about it.'

Adam added Maggie's name to the list, then put

stars by the names of people who had been confirmed. 'Anybody else?'

'Not that I know of. But until a few days ago, I didn't believe in vampires,' Jason said. 'So I guess anything's possible. What's the plan?'

'I figure we talk to people who were at the party the other night,' Adam said. 'See if anybody noticed Carrie talking to anyone on this list. That's how we narrow down our suspects.'

'But your eye is on Scott,' Jason said.

'It is. I mean, you saw them on the bed.' Adam squeezed his eyes shut as if that would block out the memory. 'But I've been thinking about it. There's no actual proof against Scott. I don't want to miss something by focusing exclusively on him.'

Jason nodded. Made sense to him. 'Aren't people going to wonder why we're so interested when we start with the questions?' he asked.

'I'll tell everyone I'm making a documentary about Carrie's death,' Adam said. 'You tell them you're helping me. People are morbid, they'll want to talk about it.'

Jason had seen *that* for himself. 'All right. I'll do what I can.' And maybe, just maybe, he thought, this investigation would keep his mind off Sienna.

* * *

'Anything?' Jason asked Adam on Thursday at lunch.

Adam shook his head. 'The usual. Everyone loved the party, no one remembers a thing about it. You ask them for specifics and their eyes glaze over.'

Jason didn't know what to say. The truth was, he had a hard time remembering anything specific from the yacht party himself. And everyone he'd talked to about Carrie's death said the same thing: they saw her making out with Scott Challon. And nothing else. 'What about Scott? He still seems to be our number-one suspect. Did your dad tell you anything new?'

'Yeah. The cops released him. The only evidence against him is circumstantial: he was the last one seen with Carrie.' Adam looked pretty wrecked. Jason wondered if he'd been sleeping at all this week. 'And it's just as we expected,' Adam went on. 'Carrie's drug tests came back, and of course they were all negative. So the police have ruled her death an accident, not murder. They're going to close the case today.'

Jason put down his pizza. Suddenly he didn't feel hungry anymore. This was so unreal. He knew Carrie had been murdered, and yet the police couldn't even prove it. Hell, they didn't even suspect murder anymore. 'I wish we could tell the police about the vampires,' he said. 'They're working without all the info.'

'Yeah, but I'd like to go to college next year,' Adam said. '"Gee, Dad, I'm pretty sure Carrie was killed by a vampire" is like a one-way ticket to a lovely padded cell.'

'Did Scott say anything to the cops?' Jason asked. 'Anything we can use?'

'Actually, he said Carrie went off with Luke Archer toward the end of the party,' Adam said.

'Luke?' Jason frowned in thought. He did remember seeing the guy there, but Luke had seemed solidly committed to his alone time with Luke. 'Did the cops talk to him?'

'Nah. My dad said they tried to, but they couldn't find him.'

'Why not?' Jason asked. 'He's been in school.'

Adam shrugged. 'Don't know. It's weird. But now that they've decided her death was accidental, they don't even care about talking to Luke. Nobody else saw Carrie with him, anyway.

'Maybe Scott was just trying to shift the blame to someone else,' Jason said thoughtfully.

'So Scott is still our prime suspect,' Adam said quietly.

Jason nodded. 'We think he's a vampire, and we definitely saw him with Carrie.'

'The police report puts Carrie's time of death at around twelve thirty,' Adam said. 'And the time stamp on my film has Carrie making out with Scott at twelve fifteen.'

'That doesn't give her much time to have gone off with Luke, or anybody else,' Jason pointed out.

'It was Scott, it had to be,' Adam said grimly. 'So that means the police have just released a bloodlusting vampire. How long do you think it's going to take for him to drain someone else?'

FOURTEEN

'Let's hit the pool, guys!' Coach Middleton yelled into the locker room after school.

Jason grabbed his towel and slammed the locker shut. Usually swim practice was his favorite part of the day – a chance to relax, work his muscles, feel the water. But today he was dreading it. He'd managed to avoid Brad all week. In fact, he'd avoided all the friends of Dracula, at least the ones he knew about.

Does Brad know Sienna told me the truth? Jason wondered. *Is he going to be pissed?* And what about the exchange they'd had at Belle's party? Jason wondered if he should apologize, maybe say he'd been drunk?

'Freeman! Let's go kick some ass,' Brad called, rounding the row of lockers. 'I'm going to set a fast time today.' He whipped his towel at Jason, hitting him in the arm, and let out a whoop. Some of the other guys picked it up, howling as they charged out to the pool.

Jason followed more slowly, not sure what to think. Brad was acting as if nothing had happened between them. Was it possible Sienna hadn't told him about her conversation with Jason?

Or did Brad just not care that Jason knew he was a vampire? Because why would he? It's not like Jason was DeVere's own Van Helsing.

'Warm up,' Coach Middleton ordered.

The guys plunged into the pool and began with some easy laps. Jason wandered over to where Brad was about to jump in.

'So, what's up?' Brad greeted him. 'Haven't seen you all week. I mean I've seen you, but you know. I can't believe it's already Thursday. I haven't even started to study for this French quiz I've got tomorrow.'

'Feels like it was Monday about three minutes ago,' Jason agreed.

'I hear ya,' said Brad. 'The first few weeks of school are always cake. But then the homework sets in and the freedom comes to an end. Sucks.' He gave Jason a grin and dove into the pool as Van Dyke climbed out, shaking water from his ear.

'Yo, Freeman!' Van Dyke bellowed, lifting Jason in a bear hug that almost crushed his ribs. Van Dyke dropped him back to the ground and ambled away.

Jason chuckled, but he couldn't help feeling a little guilty. Van Dyke had always been affable. Jason felt like an ass for holding the vampire fangs against him.

And with Brad it was even worse. He'd been nothing but a friend to Jason ever since they first met. Jason felt like a racist or something for judging Brad just because he was a vampire. It's not like the guy had a choice.

It's more than that, a little voice whispered in Jason's head. With Brad, it wasn't just the vampire issue. It was the Sienna issue. Jason felt guilty just watching Brad in the pool, knowing how he felt about the dude's girlfriend.

Sienna. How did he feel about her, anyway? Attracted to her? For sure. Disturbed by the casual way she talked about drinking blood? Also, for sure. Under the circumstances, Jason reflected, it probably wasn't safe to have feelings for her at all!

'You're up, Freeman,' Brad called. Jason started. Brad was already climbing out of the pool.

'Thanks,' Jason said. He shoved the thought of Sienna out of his head and plunged into the water.

Swimming focused him. It always did. There was no room for hot girls or vampires or a murder mystery. There was only Jason and the water and the need for speed. It was over too fast. He wished practice could last for days, long enough to let him finally get rid of all the stress the past week had generated.

But way too soon, he was out of the water and heading for the parking lot. Dani had gotten a ride today, so he would be driving home alone. And he was alone when he heard Sienna laughing. Jason didn't look up. He didn't have to, to know it was her. She was probably there to pick up Brad.

His stomach clenched into a knot. He didn't want to see Sienna, but it was unavoidable. His eyes just couldn't resist taking a look at her. Without meaning to, he stopped and glanced over.

Sienna was leaning against the adobe wall of the front stairway, laughing as Brad told her some kind of story. Jason felt his face grow hot. She never laughed that way with *him*.

'Hey, Jason. Our relay team's getting good, don't you think?' Brad called.

Great. Now Jason had to go over and join them. He had to watch as Brad slipped an arm around Sienna and she rested against him, reaching up to kiss his cheek. Whether Sienna was a vampire or not, Jason felt a surge of jealousy.

'We should be able to shave off a few more seconds

in another couple of practices,' Jason said, trying to get his mind off Brad and Sienna.

'I was thinking we should make another run to Eddie's for those fish tacos,' Brad said. He glanced at Sienna. 'Can you believe this guy ordered a beef taco there?'

Oh, don't even think about asking me to third wheel with you and Sienna, Jason thought. 'I'm not such the fish guy,' he replied.

'OK, but you and Adam and I should definitely hang out again,' Brad said. That line sounded a little rehearsed to Jason. 'Maybe we could even convince Adam to show us a little of his movie. Since we're all the stars and everything.'

That one came out even more rehearsed. *Got it*, Jason thought. Sienna must have told Brad about her conversation with Jason. Which meant Brad knew that Adam was on to them, that his movie was about the vampires, and now Brad was worried that Adam might tell other people what he knew.

Just like he was the first day we hit Eddie's! Jason realized. Brad had seen Adam filming the big guy that Dominic had pulverized. He knew that it was totally fishy that Dominic had beaten up a guy the size of a house, so he didn't want Adam talking to Sam. That explained Brad's sudden change of plan and his sudden interest in hanging with Jason and Adam. Jason chuckled. He was finally starting to understand a lot of things.

'You think Adam would be up for that?' Brad asked. Even Sienna looked a little anxious about the answer. Jason decided to tell them what they really wanted to know: whether Adam was against them or not.

'I doubt he'd be willing to show the masterpiece until it's done,' Jason replied. 'But I know he'd be up for a taco run. He's always telling me how long he's known you – you and Sienna and everyone. He's a fan.'

The unasked question had been answered. Brad smiled. Sienna relaxed.

'Cool. I'll text you,' Brad told Jason. He slid his arm from Sienna's shoulders to her waist. 'Catch you later.'

'Bye, Jason,' Sienna said, giving him a long, serious look as she headed off with Brad. But it wasn't enough. A few words and a meaningful look was just not enough of Sienna.

I've got to see her alone, Jason thought. *Even if she is a vampire.*

'Red alert,' Adam said, coming up to Jason in the walkway at the end of Friday afternoon. 'I got a tip.'

'Yeah? What?' Jason asked.

'I followed Scott into the bathroom after physics. Heard him making plans to go out tonight. I'm going to trail him, see if he tries to pick up a girl.'

Damn, Jason thought. He'd been planning to go to Sienna's after school, but he didn't want to tell Adam that. He'd never admitted to his friend that he had a huge crush on Sienna.

'You think you'll be OK without me?' he asked Adam. 'I have a thing tonight.'

'Oh. Yeah, sure,' Adam said. He didn't sound all that confident, though.

'Listen, all you're going to do is follow him, right?' Jason asked. 'You're not going to try to fight him or anything.'

'Right,' Adam said.

'If you need me to play Robin the Boy Wonder, call me on my cell and I'll get your back,' Jason told him as they walked out to the parking lot.

'You know it.' Adam split off toward his Vespa, while Jason headed for the VW.

Dani was waiting for him. 'Thank God it's the weekend,' she said as soon as he got in the car. 'I am so sick of getting up when it's still dark out.'

'Yeah,' Jason murmured, pulling out of the lot.

'Kristy and I are going to this barbeque tomorrow – Alexa Vassard is throwing it. Apparently Alexa's parents have the biggest hot tub in Malibu,' Dani said.

'Uh-huh.' Jason never bothered to listen when Dani talked about her plans. He was just happy to hear her back in social mode. Maybe she was going to like it in California after all. He let her chatter on while he thought about what to say to Sienna.

He knew it was a little eccentric to just show up at her house like nothing had happened. Still, it wasn't exactly as if they'd had a fight . . .

'Is that Scott Challon's brother?' Dani asked.

The mention of Scott's name caught Jason's attention. 'Huh?' he queried, looking around. He'd stopped at a red light, but he hadn't noticed the car that had pulled up beside him. Dani nodded toward it, trying to be subtle. 'You know, Scott, the guy the cops thought—'

'Yeah, I know Scott,' Jason interrupted. He leaned forward so he could see past Dani into the vintage Mustang next to them. Luke Archer was at the wheel, lost in his own world as usual. He didn't even glance in their direction.

The light changed, and Jason hit the gas. 'That was Luke Archer,' he told Dani. 'He's not Scott's brother.'

'Are they cousins or something?'

'No.' Jason squinted at his sister. 'Why?'

'They look so much alike,' Dani commented, as she pulled her bag onto her lap and began digging through it for something. Obviously she was done with the conversation. But Jason was stuck on the Scott and Luke thing.

'They don't look anything alike,' he said. 'Scott's a jock, and Luke's a . . . I don't know, a loner.'

Dani rolled her eyes. 'That has nothing to do with what they look like.'

'I know, it's just that they're really different. Luke's thin and pale and stuff.'

'They have the same hair,' Dani said. 'Same basic chin and cheekbones.'

'If you say so,' Jason replied doubtfully. 'Obviously you spend way more time looking at guys than I do.'

Dani swatted at him and he laughed.

After he'd dropped her off at home, Jason headed straight over to Sienna's house. He wanted to get there before he chickened out. If he was going to see her, he had to do it now. He had to know what was between them. Did she feel anything for him? Did he pull at her heart the way she did at his? And did that even matter?

Did anything matter other than the harsh fact that she used his kind for food?

Jason leaped out of the car, strode to the door, and rang the bell. He was hoping Sienna would answer, but he figured he could deal with her mom again if he had to.

He wasn't expecting Zach Lafrenière.

'Freeman,' Zach said, sounding less than thrilled. He looked Jason up and down with his cool dark eyes, radiating a faint air of disapproval. Even so, Jason couldn't help feeling as if he wanted Zach on his side. There was something about the guy that caught your attention. He was all coiled energy, like a snake ready to strike.

'Hey, Zach,' Jason said. 'I'm looking for Sienna.'

Zach didn't move. He held Jason's gaze for a moment, his dark eyes boring into Jason as if he could read his mind. *He knows*, Jason realized. *He knows Sienna told me about them.* But he didn't break eye contact. Even though his heart was racing, he didn't want Zach to know he was on edge.

This guy is a vampire, Jason thought. But the idea was still too Sci-Fi Channel to feel real.

'Sienna!' Zach called suddenly. Then he nodded briefly to Jason, turned and walked away, leaving the door open. It wasn't exactly an invitation, but it wasn't a get-the-hell-outta-here, either. Jason stepped inside and followed Zach toward the backyard.

Sienna was just getting up from her chaise when Jason reached the glass doors. His heart sank as he took in the scene: not just Zach, but Brad, Van Dyke, Belle, Dominic and Erin. They all sat around the pool, just hanging out like normal people. Except that they were all vampires. Sienna hadn't confirmed his suspicions about Belle and Dominic, but Jason was pretty sure that this group had more in common than just the fact that they were cool and rich.

Jason was alone in a house full of blood-drinkers and something primal inside was screaming at him to run. But Sienna was walking toward him, a smile playing on her lips, her dark eyes as intoxicating as ever. Jason felt he knew her; she wasn't evil.

He forced himself to act normally as he stood by the doors, waiting for Sienna to reach him.

'Jason,' Sienna said. 'Hi. Do you want to join us?'

He took a deep breath. 'Maybe. What you doing?'

Belle and Zach exchanged a look. Van Dyke suddenly got up and jumped into the pool, swimming furiously.

'Nothing,' Sienna said. 'Just hanging.'

But everyone was quiet and tense. Jason had clearly interrupted something. He glanced at Zach again. Zach didn't look away. 'No thanks,' Jason said. 'I just wanted to drop by and say hello. So, hello, and now I'll let you get back to . . . hanging.'

He turned back into the house, and Sienna followed him to the front door.

'What was that all about?' he asked her quietly.

She sighed. 'Look—'

'Did I interrupt some big vampire conference?'

'We're trying to figure out what happened to Carrie,' Sienna murmured, glancing over her shoulder. 'I told you, Zach wants to take care of it.'

'Well, good luck.' Jason reached for the doorknob.

'Wait,' Sienna said, stepping closer to him. 'I'm glad you came. I didn't expect to see you here again.'

The closeness of her made his head swim. 'I didn't expect to be here again,' he admitted, smiling in spite of himself. 'But I had to see you.'

Sienna smiled back, and took another step toward him, and immediately Jason felt himself swept away – by her apple-vanilla scent that reminded him of the ocean, the wild, vivid beauty of her face and the incredible sweetness of her smile. If he didn't touch her, he thought he might go crazy. Without thinking, Jason reached out and slipped his arm around her waist, pulling her close. Before he could stop himself, his mouth was on hers.

He felt Sienna's body tense in surprise, but then slowly her arms moved up around his neck. She opened her lips, inviting him in, deepening the kiss, her tongue, briefly, meeting his.

Then, abruptly, she pulled away. Her dark eyes troubled now, confused.

Jason smiled, turned and left the house. He felt Sienna watching him as he walked to his VW and got in. And he couldn't stop himself from grinning; it was nice to know that Sienna was just as confused about their relationship as he was.

He was still too wired to head home, so he went for a drive. It was great to be living in a state where he could actually make use of having a convertible, even in the fall. The sun on the ocean was dazzling as he sped along the Pacific Coast Highway. In the water, he could see a few surfers making the most of the late-afternoon sunshine.

Jason breathed in the salty ocean air and felt himself begin to unwind. There'd been a weird vibe over at Sienna's, no doubt, but no one had threatened him. No fangs had made an appearance. It was probably just like

Sienna said – the vampires were talking about their rogue member, whoever he was. Trying to figure out what to do. Trying to help. But they clearly didn't want an outsider like him getting involved.

By the time Jason turned back towards DeVere Heights, the last rays of the sun were turning the sea to gold. Jason's cell rang. He glanced at the number: Adam.

'How's it going?' Jason asked as soon as he hit TALK.

'We've got a problem.' Adam sounded freaked.

'What?'

'It's Scott. He just went into The Dreamhouse.'

'Where?' Jason asked.

'It's a club in town. But that's not the problem. Jason, he had a girl with him. What if he's going to kill her?'

FIFTEEN

Jason pulled over to the side of the road. He needed to concentrate. 'Calm down,' he told Adam. 'How do you know she's not some friend of his – another vampire, even?'

'I've never seen her before,' Adam said. 'And besides, he just picked her up on Santa Monica Pier. That's where he went after school. He met her there, they started flirting, then they went to The Dreamhouse together.'

Jason's throat felt tight. 'If he wanted to kill her, why wouldn't he just take her to an alley or something?' he asked.

'I don't know, maybe he likes the thrill,' Adam spat. 'He didn't kill Carrie in some dark alley.'

'Good point,' Jason acknowledged. He figured The Dreamhouse was probably pretty dark and crowded, just like Belle's yacht had been. Nobody had noticed Carrie's death there, and nobody would notice another girl's death at the club. 'All right, look, we don't know for sure that Scott is the rogue vampire,' he said, as much to reassure himself as Adam. 'I'll meet you at the club and we'll watch him together. If it seems like he's going to bite anyone, we'll stop him.'

'How are we going to get in?' Adam asked. 'We're not legal.'

'Don't worry, it'll be fine,' Jason said, hoping that was true. 'Just wait for me.'

He hung up and pulled the VW back out onto the road. He didn't plan to drink tonight, but he figured he'd better leave the car at home just in case. Luckily, his parents were out at a business dinner for the evening, so he didn't have to explain where he was going in such a rush.

'Dani!' he yelled as he tossed the car keys onto the counter.

No answer.

'Danielle?' He glanced around and spotted a giant pink Post-it on the fridge. He grabbed it and read, 'Gone to Kristy's to study. May sleep over. Dani, XOXO.'

'Huh. That better be the truth,' Jason muttered. He didn't want to think about her out at some party, being a nice snack for a vampire. He called a cab, changed into jeans and a black T-shirt, and ran back outside just as the cab arrived.

It took ten minutes to get to The Dreamhouse. Adam was waiting out front. 'How are we going to get in? I don't have a fake I.D.,' he said anxiously.

'I'm not sure. Let's just go check it out.' Jason strode confidently to the door. At every club he'd ever been to, he'd found that if you just looked like you knew what you were doing, they'd let you in. Hopefully it would be the same here. 'Hey,' he said to the bouncer, his eyes already roaming the inside of the club to show that he wasn't nervous about being carded. 'Two of us. What's the cover?'

'Hey, Freeman. Ten bucks each.' Jason looked up in surprise. The bouncer was Luke Archer!

'Luke, thank God,' Adam said. 'I was worried we wouldn't get in.'

Luke cracked a smile and glanced around. 'No worries,' he said. 'You still have to pay, though.'

Jason handed over a twenty, taking in Luke's muscular arms. He'd never noticed before how built the guy was. Luke wasn't on any sports teams, so Jason had always kind of assumed he wasn't athletic. But obviously he worked out – maybe so he could keep this job. You couldn't be a bouncer unless you were big enough to be intimidating.

'Thanks, man,' he said. Luke nodded.

The club was packed. It was a different crowd from the parties in DeVere Heights, mostly college-age kids. The lights were dim. House music pulsed through huge speakers on the walls, and the tiny dance floor was crowded with writhing bodies. Deep booths lined the sides of the place, big enough for six or seven people to sit. In the back room there was a pool table – though nothing close to the museum piece at Brad's – and a few dartboards.

Jason pushed his way through the crowd, scanning the faces for Scott Challon. Adam followed, peering at the people in the deep booths. At the back of the room, Jason spotted a wide double-door. It led out onto a huge deck over the beach. People hung around in little clumps out here, smoking and talking away from the loud music inside. He did a quick check for Scott, but there was no sign of the guy.

'Let's go back inside,' Adam said. 'Scott's not out here.'

'Yeah.' Jason went back in and led the way over to the other side of the room.

'There he is,' Adam murmured.

Jason followed his friend's gaze and spotted Scott.

He sat in a corner booth, all the way at the back, his arm around a pretty red-haired girl. A few other guys sat toward the front of the booth, playing some drinking game. Jason thought he recognized them from school, but it was hard to see them clearly in the dark of the club.

'Grab that table,' he told Adam, pointing to a small table about fifteen feet from Scott's booth. 'We'll hang here and keep an eye on him.'

'What are we going to do if he attacks her?' Adam asked. 'He's got friends with him. We can't take them all.'

'Buffalo, buffalo, buffalo!' the guys at Scott's table began to chant.

'Hopefully he won't attack her,' Jason said, raising his voice to be heard over the buffalo boys. 'If he does, we make a scene, get everybody looking in his direction. He won't do anything public.'

Adam nodded. 'I wish I had my camera,' he said. 'Then I could get proof.'

Jason laughed. 'I don't think the club owners would appreciate you filming a high-school kid hanging out in their place.' He stood up. 'I'm going to get some beers so they don't come kick us out.' He made his way back through the crowd to the long wooden bar. It was near the entrance, so he glanced over at Luke to nod hello. But Luke didn't notice – his attention was focused somewhere toward the back of the place. Jason turned to follow his line of sight, and was surprised to see that Luke was watching Scott Challon.

'Help you?' the girl behind the bar yelled over the music.

Jason turned, taking in her platinum-blond pigtails and her pierced eyebrow. 'Yeah, uh, two Super Bocks.'

She grabbed a couple of bottles, opened them and handed them over. Jason dropped some cash on the bar and picked up the beers. He glanced back at Luke, but there was some other beefy dude at the door now. *Must be Luke's breaktime*, Jason decided as he elbowed his way through the crowd. But at the edge of the dance floor, he spotted Luke again. Not dancing, not even talking to anyone, just standing there – and he was still watching Scott Challon.

'Check it,' Jason said, setting the beers on the table. He nodded over his shoulder to Luke.

'What?' Adam asked.

'Luke's been eyeballing Scott the entire time I was gone,' Jason told him. 'You think he's suspicious, too?'

Adam shrugged. 'Could be. He may not suspect Scott's a vampire, but Scott did try to shift the blame for Carrie's death onto Luke. Maybe Luke heard about that and wants to make sure Scott gets taken downtown.'

'Yeah. Or maybe he's seen Scott here before,' Jason said grimly. 'Maybe he's seen him pick up other girls – or hurt them.'

Luke suddenly turned away and headed toward the back of the club.

'I'm going to follow him,' Jason said. 'Maybe he can tell us something useful.'

'You're not going to say anything about vampires, are you?' Adam asked anxiously.

'No, I'll just see if I can get him talking about Scott,' Jason said. 'If he's suspicious of the guy, he might mention something we don't know.'

'Sounds good. I'll stay here and keep an eye on that girl. And the vampire she's sitting with!' Adam took a swig of his beer and settled into his seat.

Jason headed toward the back of the club again, peering through the bodies for any sign of Luke. How could he lose sight of such a big guy? But Luke was gone. Jason glanced out onto the deck. No sign of him. He wasn't near the pool table, either. The only other place was the men's room. Jason pushed open the swing door and went in.

It was even darker in here – two out of three lights were broken – but it only took Jason a few moments to realize that the room was empty, except for Scott Challon.

Jason was so surprised to see Scott that he just stared.

'Hey,' Scott said, catching his eye in the mirror.

Jason recovered quickly. 'Hey,' he said, making sure to sound bored. He ambled over to the sinks, where Scott was checking his hair in the mirror. Jason turned on the water, splashed some on his face, then ran his hand through his own hair. He glanced at the stalls, just to see if Luke had gone into one of them, but there was nobody there.

He gave Scott a nod and went back out into the club. Immediately, he scanned the crowd for Adam, expecting him to have followed Scott over. There was a thin, sandy-haired guy playing darts, but when he turned toward the dim lights, Jason could see it wasn't his friend. Where was Adam?

A sudden fear struck him – what if Scott had jumped Adam as soon as he was alone? It would've been easy enough for Scott to spot Adam watching him.

How long does it take a vampire to kill someone? Jason wondered frantically. Sienna hadn't told him that. He shoved his way through the crowd, desperate to get back to his table. If Adam wasn't there . . .

But Adam *was* there. Converse sneakers up on the neighboring chair, drinking his beer as if nothing was wrong. Jason let out a sigh of relief, and dropped into his chair.

Adam gave him a once-over. 'You look like crap, my friend,' he commented.

'Why are you still here?' Jason asked. 'You were supposed to be following Scott.'

'I *am* following Scott.' Adam raised his beer toward the corner booth. 'He hasn't moved.'

'What?' Jason squinted across the room at Scott Challon, who was sitting exactly where he'd been when Jason left. Scott's arm was still around the redhead, and now they were kissing.

'So far it's been pretty tame,' Adam said. 'He hasn't gone anywhere near her neck. Or arm. Or looked like biting her at all. The second he does, I figure I'll hurl my beer bottle at him. That should get everyone's attention.'

'But—' Jason stopped, baffled. 'Are you sure he didn't get up at all?'

SIXTEEN

Jason was beginning to wonder if he was losing his mind. He'd just been in the bathroom with Scott, not Luke. He was certain of it. And yet, here was Scott, sitting where he'd been sitting all evening and Adam said he hadn't moved! Jason glanced across to see that Luke was back working the door. This was getting confusing.

Dani said Scott and Luke look alike, he reminded himself. *Guess she was right.*

'Here we go,' Adam said. 'Scott's getting up.'

Jason spun back toward the corner booth. Scott was inching his way along the bench to get up. His friends were already standing, waiting for him. The redhead slid along the bench behind him.

'We've got to follow them,' Adam said, moving to get up too.

'Wait a sec. I don't think the girl's going with them,' Jason replied. 'Look.' The red-haired girl was writing on Scott's hand with a ballpoint pen. *Probably giving him her number*, Jason thought. She stood on her tiptoes and kissed Scott, then wandered off into the crowd.

Scott and his buddies headed for the door.

'Still, we have to go after him,' Adam insisted. 'He might go pick up another girl somewhere else.'

Jason nodded slowly. Adam was right. But his confusion between Scott and Luke was still bothering him. 'You go ahead,' he told Adam. 'I'm going to stay here. I want to keep an eye on Luke.'

'Luke?' Adam repeated. 'Why? He's not a suspect. He's not even a vampire!'

'I know, but there's something strange going on,' Jason said. 'I can't explain it.'

'If anything, Luke's on our side,' Adam pointed out. 'He seems to suspect Scott, too.'

'You're going to lose Scott if you don't go now,' Jason said.

'OK.' Adam gave him one last, confused look. 'You sure you want to stay here?'

'Yeah. Call me if anything bad happens.'

Adam nodded and went off after Scott. Jason saw him slap hands with Luke on the way out. Luke was looking perfectly relaxed as if everything was normal.

Which it probably was.

Jason went over to the bar and found a seat. He ordered another beer and settled down to watch Luke, feeling like an idiot. Adam was right. Luke had always seemed like a pretty normal guy, and Jason had no reason to suspect him of anything. In fact, he didn't even know what he *did* suspect. But there was an uneasy feeling in his stomach, and it had something to do with Luke.

'What time does this place close?' he asked the pigtailed bartender.

'Two,' she answered. 'Why? Are you in it for the long haul?'

'I think so,' he replied, glancing at his watch. It was only midnight, and Luke was probably working the door until closing.

Jason turned on his stool to look out over the whole club. The redhead who'd been with Scott was now dancing with a group of girls on the dance floor. Luke was leaning against the doorframe, taking money and checking IDs. Jason sighed and took a sip of beer. It was going to be a long night.

At one-thirty, the red-haired girl brushed past him, heading for the door. Jason watched her go, hoping she didn't plan to meet up with Scott. He pulled out his cell and checked for messages. Nothing. He hadn't heard from Adam since he left.

When he looked up again, Luke was gone.

Jason leaped off his stool and rushed over to the door. Just outside, he could see Luke talking to the other bouncer. The other guy nodded, then they banged fists in farewell and Luke took off toward the parking lot.

Surprised, Jason followed him. *How am I supposed to trail him without a car?* he wondered. Jason smiled wryly. He wasn't too great at this detective stuff. Guess he'd never grow up to be a private eye. But he could at least see what direction Luke drove off in.

He kept back twenty feet or more, not wanting Luke to notice he was being followed. Luke walked all the way to the edge of the parking lot, where there were no lights, and faded into the darkness behind a huge H2.

Jason broke into a jog, trying to catch up. When he reached the SUV, he stopped and inched his way around it, using it for cover.

There! Luke was leaning against a Toyota – who knew they allowed Toyotas in Malibu? – five feet away. But he wasn't alone. The redhead from the club was with him, keys dangling from her hand as she laughed at something Luke said.

The Toyota must be her car, Jason thought. *But what is she doing with Luke?*

Their voices were low, so he couldn't make out the words, but the tone was clearly flirtatious. Jason shook his head. He figured this was the reason why Luke had been watching Scott – Scott was hitting on the girl he liked! It didn't explain the men's-room confusion, of course, but it had been dark in there. Jason decided he'd just made a mistake – and he felt like kicking himself; he'd hung out here all night in order to watch a guy who was just jealous!

He almost felt like laughing. Between Sienna telling him about the vampires and Adam getting so caught up in his investigation of Scott, Jason's mind was spinning. He'd seriously started imagining things – like Luke turning into Scott Challon in the bathroom.

I'm going to call a cab to go home, he decided. *I've had enough of playing Van Helsing for one night.*

'Come on,' Luke's voice broke into his thoughts. 'The view is great from there.'

Jason plastered himself against the H2, hoping they wouldn't see him. He didn't want to have to explain to Luke why he was hanging out in the middle of a deserted parking lot.

'From the alley?' The girl sounded skeptical.

'No. The entrance is in the alley,' Luke said. 'There's a gate that leads to the beach.'

'OK. Sounds delicious.' The girl giggled, and Jason heard their footsteps moving away toward the service alley that ran behind the club. He peered around the other side of the SUV, waiting for them to move out of sight so that he could show himself.

The moon had come out from behind a cloud, and it shone down onto the lot. He could see the girl clearly now, see her smile as she adjusted her purse on her shoulder.

And he could see the guy, too – which came as something of a shock. Because it wasn't Luke Archer.

It was Scott Challon.

SEVENTEEN

'Let's go,' Scott said. He took the girl's hand and led her toward the alley.

Jason had to remind himself to breathe. What was Scott doing back at the club? Where had he come from? Jason scanned the parking lot, looking for Adam. Surely his friend would have called him to say Scott was heading back to The Dreamhouse.

But it was Luke with that girl, a voice whispered in Jason's head. He had been certain that it was Luke. It made no sense. How could the girl be with Luke one second and with Scott the next?

She couldn't be, Jason thought. *Unless Luke made himself look like Scott!*

And, with that thought, Jason yanked out his cell and called Adam, who answered on the first ring.

'Adam, where's Scott?' Jason demanded. 'You still following him?'

'Yeah. He's at Duke's Burgers. Been here for more

than an hour,' Adam complained. 'Just him and his friends. I wish they'd go home if they're not going to commit any crimes.'

Jason's heart was thumping so hard he was surprised Adam couldn't hear it. 'You're sure he's there right now?'

'Yes. He's eating French fries and telling jokes. His boys are laughing. I'm looking right at him.'

'So am I,' Jason murmured. 'Scott and that redhead he was with earlier have just disappeared around the side of the club.'

'*What?*' Adam cried.

'Just stay on Scott. Don't let him leave your sight,' Jason said. He hung up the phone and ran toward the alley. He thought he knew what was going on now, and it was very, very bad. If Scott was sitting in a burger bar, then it had to be Luke holding hands with the redhead. And there was only one way that Luke could have made himself look like Scott Challon: he had to be a vampire.

Jason raced around The Dreamhouse and into the alley. It was darker here – the moon was blocked by the two-storey building and there were no lights. The sound of the surf drifted up from the beach behind the alley, but Jason had a hard time believing there was any beach access from back here. The alley was filled with dumpsters for the club and some old rusted bar stools. Besides The Dreamhouse, the nearest building was three hundred yards away. There was absolutely no reason for anyone to come into this alley, unless they were here to drop off supplies at the service entrance to the club, or to pick up the garbage. Why would anyone bother putting in an access path to the beach?

He's going to kill her, Jason thought with absolute certainty. Soft laughter drifted toward him from somewhere up ahead. He hurried forward, running softly to keep from being heard. Finally he spotted them, up against the concrete wall of the club, making out. Luke's hands were in her red hair, and his lips were on her neck. He opened his mouth, and Jason saw the moonlight glint off vicious fangs as plunged them into the girl's flesh.

Jason shouted, 'Hey!' and the vampire looked up.

He still looked like Scott Challon in almost every way. But his eyes met Jason's. Green eyes, shining in the darkness, as if they were lit from within. There was no humanity there, only evil and uncontrolled desire: bloodlust. This was what Sienna had described – pure, pulsating hunger for human blood. There was nothing behind those eyes except an unnatural need. But of one thing Jason was completely certain: they were Luke Archer's eyes.

Jason actually felt a momentary sense of relief as everything finally added up. It had been Luke all along. He'd been impersonating Scott the whole time – even at Belle's yacht party – and so Scott had gotten arrested, not Luke. No one had even seen Luke near the dead girl. Well, except Scott, Jason remembered, but nobody had believed him.

Luke was staring at Jason now, his fangs still sunk into the skin of the girl's neck.

'I think we've got some things to discuss,' Jason said firmly. He took a step toward the vampire.

Luke lifted his head, and released the girl's neck. Blood dripped from the corner of his mouth, black as oil in the darkness. The redhead swooned, falling back against the wall of the club, almost unconscious. She raised her hand to her neck, smearing blood all over herself. But when she saw it on her fingers, she only laughed as if it was the funniest thing she'd ever seen.

'Get out of here!' Jason told her. 'Run. *Go!*

The girl looked up at him, still smiling vaguely as if she'd had too much nitrous oxide at the dentist's surgery.

'*Run!*' Jason yelled.

She blinked, confused, then turned to Luke. 'Scott, what's going on?' she asked.

Luke smiled, his razor-sharp fangs showing white against the darkness. His eyes still glowed with lust. 'It's your lucky day,' he hissed at the girl.

Finally she seemed to snap out of her trance. Staring at the atrocity that was Luke's mouth, she backed away. Jason grabbed her arms and shoved her toward the entrance of the alley. Tears streaking her face, she stumbled into a run. He watched her until she disappeared around the corner of the building. Then he turned to face the vampire.

Luke licked his lips and smiled a bloody smile. 'It's nice of you to take her place,' he growled, his voice at least an octave lower than normal. 'I generally prefer female blood, but if it means so much to you, I'll be happy to drink yours instead.'

EIGHTEEN

Jason felt a thrill of fear as he stared at the creature before him: a *vampire*. It was like a fever nightmare come to life.

Luke chuckled. The sound was grating, like metal scraping against metal. And somehow it cleared through the fog of fear in Jason's brain. No matter *what* the guy was, he'd killed an innocent girl. And he intended to kill again. Jason wasn't about to let that happen.

'Sorry. I'm not up for getting drained by a blood-lusting freak tonight,' he said grimly.

Luke's laughter echoed off the walls of the building as he began to change. His face twisted, losing any hint of Scott Challon's features. Gradually, the face of Luke Archer emerged. The same face that Luke wore when he sat at Jason's lunch table in the school cafeteria. But then his body began to change, as well. The muscles of his arms expanded, growing to twice their normal size.

His legs and torso lengthened. Even his neck seemed to stretch as he grew half a foot taller, so that he now towered over Jason.

Finally Luke stood still – impossibly strong, improbably massive. His upper lip curled and he let out a low snarl.

Jason's neck spasmed as if his body remembered the last fight he'd had with a vampire – Dominic. The guy had been kind of thin, and not very muscular, but he'd almost squeezed Jason's throat closed before Jason had managed to defend himself. His strength had been entirely out of proportion to his size.

But Luke was huge. Jason couldn't even imagine how strong he was. He swallowed hard and balled his hands into fists. There was no way to escape. All he could do was fight.

Jason went on the offensive, dropping into a fighting stance and then springing forward with a series of jabs to Luke's torso. He got in a few solid hits, but the guy barely seemed to notice. He grabbed Jason's hand in mid-swing and jerked him forward, toward those flashing fangs.

Jason's old ju-jitsu training cut in, and he ducked, still going forward, using the force of Luke's own move against him. Luke stumbled backwards, thrown off balance. Jason took advantage of the vampire's confusion to get in a roundhouse kick to the chest. Luke stumbled even further back.

But then he laughed. In one move, he lunged forward and backhanded Jason across the face. The blow was so strong that Jason's head snapped to the side and he fell. Luke was on him immediately, pinning Jason to the ground. He bared his fangs. 'Did you really think you could stop me?' he snarled.

'No . . . But I can,' a cold voice replied.

Luke leaped off Jason and scanned the alley.

Jason looked around curiously, too, as he scrambled to his feet. But there was nobody there; nobody had entered the alley. And yet, by the time he turned back to Luke, Zach Lafrenière stood between them.

Jason glanced up at the roof of the club. Zach must have jumped down from there. Insane. The thing had to be almost thirty feet high. As if ordinary guys morphing into muscle-bound heavyweights wasn't enough, now it seemed vampires could also jump like cats!

Jason watched the two vampires as they faced off.

Luke didn't bother talking to Zach. He just hurled himself at the other vampire. But Zach leaped straight up into the air, tumbling over Luke's shoulder to land behind him. Immediately he wrapped his arm around the bigger guy's neck and squeezed.

Jason backed away, trying to get out of the range of Luke's flailing legs. Luke was struggling, twisting back and forth, but Zach held on. Finally Luke threw all his weight back against the wall of the club, slamming Zach into the concrete.

Zach let out a strangled cry, and Luke laughed and jerked away from Zach's grasp, turning to attack head-on. But Zach was still faster than him. He ducked and rolled to the side, so that Luke's fist smashed harmlessly into the wall.

Behind his opponent once again, Zach jumped into the air, shooting six feet straight up. He kicked Luke in the back of the neck, snapping his head forward. Then, on the way down, he caught hold of the guy's head and twisted it savagely to one side, trying to break his neck. Watching, Jason felt as if he'd slipped into *The Matrix*. The usual laws of physics just didn't seem to apply to vampires.

Luke spun with the move and grabbed Zach's legs, using the force of Zach's jump against him. Zach flew through the air and landed in a heap ten feet away.

Jason expected him to stay there, but Zach leaped right back up and charged at Luke, slamming him against one of the dumpsters. The thick metal crumpled where he hit it. Thick. Metal. Crumpled. Jason could hardly believe what he was seeing.

Luke bellowed like an enraged animal. He pummeled Zach with his fists, his eyes burning like green fire. Zach blocked most of the blows, but he was slowing down.

He hasn't drunk as much blood as Luke, Jason realized. *That blood consumed in bloodlust has made Luke stronger.*

Zach ducked a blow and jumped to the side, grabbing one of the rusted bar stools. He held it in front of him for protection, but Luke caught hold of the metal legs and pulled with all his strength. Zach flew forward, stumbling to the ground as Luke tore the stool from his grasp.

In one move, Luke snapped a metal leg off the stool and hurled himself on top of his enemy. Pinning Zach down with one arm, he raised the metal leg over his head like a spear. In just a moment, Luke would plunge the metal stake into Zach's heart, and Jason was pretty sure Sienna had said that that was fatal for humans and vampires alike.

He didn't think. He just ran at Luke and threw himself at the vampire with all his strength.

Caught off guard, Luke was thrown off of Zach, just as he had started to bring the metal stake down. He hit the ground hard, and Jason heard the stake clatter to the pavement. He breathed a sigh of relief; he'd saved Zach's life – for the time being. But right now was not the time to celebrate.

Hold him down, Jason told himself, driving Luke's shoulders into the ground with every ounce of strength he possessed. But in a few moments, Luke had managed to free one arm. He reached up and threw Jason off. Jason felt himself flying through the air and then he slammed into the blacktop – hard. The wind was forced from his lungs, and he lay still for a moment, trying to catch his breath.

Meanwhile, Luke rose to his feet, reached down and grabbed Jason by the throat. He lifted him off the ground with one hand and slammed him back against the wall. Jason kicked out, hoping to connect with a vulnerable part of Luke, but there didn't seem to be one.

Jason couldn't think of another plan of attack because he was suspended several feet above the ground and finding it hard to breathe. He struggled to stay conscious, but blackness clouded his vision. All he could see were Luke's blazing green eyes as he bared his fangs and went for Jason's jugular.

Then there was a sickening thud, followed by a hideous sucking sound. Luke's eyes widened in surprise and he looked down. Jason followed his gaze – just in time to see the metal stake emerge from Luke's ribcage and shoot straight into the wall beneath his own armpit.

Luke stared at the metal stake in confusion. Then he slumped forward, dead.

Over Luke's hunched shoulders, Jason met Zach's eyes. His gaze was cool and steady, in spite of the fact that he had just stabbed Luke through the heart.

Was he trying to stab us both? Jason wondered.

Zach jerked the stake backwards, and Luke's body tumbled to the pavement. Jason fell with him, landing in a crouch over the vampire. But he didn't take his eyes off the body, because it was changing. The crazed vampire who'd been ready to kill Jason a few seconds ago was gone. Luke was . . . Luke again. A thin guy, not especially tall, not especially muscular.

But, Jason realized, there was something else different about him now – his features seemed sharper, his bone structure more perfect, his skin completely unblemished. He'd never been this remarkable looking at school. Clearly he'd been toning down his appearance the same way Sienna did, in order to blend in.

His clear green eyes were open, but the crazed glow of the bloodlust was gone. His mouth bore traces of blood, but the fangs had vanished. He looked entirely human.

'Freeman.' Jason looked up to see Zach holding out a hand. He grabbed it and Zach pulled him to his feet. 'You OK?'

'Yeah.' Jason's voice came out hoarse. He looked down at himself, searching for signs of injury. Everything hurt, but nothing seemed to be broken. 'I'm fine.' He looked at Zach. 'How about you?'

Zach laughed, but there was no humor in it. 'I'm great,' he said. And Jason could see that he was. The guy looked as if he was going clubbing, not as if he'd just survived the fight of his life. No bruises, no blood, not a hair out of place.

'What were you doing here?' Jason asked.

'Looking for him.' Zach glanced down at Luke. 'We couldn't let him kill again.'

'You knew?' Jason demanded. 'You knew it was Luke?'

'Not until tonight,' Zach said. 'He didn't grow up with us, so we didn't know he was . . . one of us. But there's a certain feeling we get. I've had suspicions about him for a while now.'

'And you didn't do anything about it?' Jason said, disgusted.

'I didn't know he'd go rogue,' Zach replied flatly. 'Bloodlust is dangerous. It's forbidden. We're taught that almost from infancy. None of us would ever give in to it. The very idea is unthinkable.'

Jason sighed. 'Sorry. I know you're not all . . . like him. I'm just—'

'It's all right,' Zach cut him off.

Jason studied him. Sienna and Brad were so friendly, so *normal*. But Zach was different. Aloof. Yet he'd done the right thing tonight.

'You saved my life,' Jason said. 'I guess I owe you one.'

'No. You saved my life too,' Zach said. 'You don't owe me anything.'

Jason smiled. 'OK. We're even.'

For the first time, Zach smiled back. For an instant, then it was gone. 'No, not even. You shouldn't have been here. It wasn't your problem,' he said. 'Go home. I've got some cleaning up to do.'

Jason blinked in surprise. Cleaning up? Weren't they going to call the cops? What the hell was Zach going to do with a dead guy who'd been staked through the heart? He opened his mouth to ask, but the look on Zach's face silenced him.

I don't want to know, Jason decided. He already knew more about the ways of vampires than he wanted to. 'OK. Good luck,' Jason said.

Zach just raised an eyebrow.

'Right. No luck necessary,' Jason corrected himself. He turned and walked away. Zach obviously knew what he was doing.

When he got back to the parking lot, Jason pulled out his cell and called Adam.

'Jason? What's going on?' Adam greeted him.

'You still following Scott?' Jason asked, picking his way through the cars toward the road.

'Yeah.'

'Well, you can stop,' Jason said. 'We found the killer—'

'*We?*' Adam interrupted.

'It's a long story. I'll tell you tomorrow.' Jason reached the edge of the parking lot and stepped out onto the sidewalk. It was late, and only a few cars whizzed by on the Pacific Coast Highway.

'So it's not Scott?' Adam asked.

'No. It was Luke Archer. He was a vampire,' Jason said. 'But he's dead.'

There was a long silence on the other end of the line. 'Jason,' Adam finally said. 'Did you—?'

'No.' Jason took a deep breath. 'Look. It's all taken care of. I'll explain in the morning.'

'Wanna meet at Peet's Coffee?'

'Yeah. I'll see you there at ten.' Jason hit END, then began scrolling through his phone book for the number of the cab company he'd used to get to the club. He felt drained, both physically and mentally, as if he'd been through a twelve-round boxing match and the SATs all at once.

'Need a lift?'

The voice was unmistakable: *Sienna.* Jason looked up slowly from his phone, unable to stop himself from smiling at the sight of her. The exhaustion vanished from his body the instant his eyes met hers.

She sat in her Spider, which was idling on the side of the road. 'What are you doing here?' he asked, walking over. He leaned in through the passenger side window.

'I was at the The Dreamhouse,' Sienna said.

'Not while I was in there, you weren't,' Jason replied.

She shrugged. 'Maybe you just didn't see me.'

He squinted at her. Was she saying she'd changed her appearance, too? Or was she just teasing him? 'Did you come with Zach?' he asked.

Sienna switched her attention to the CD player, and changed the disc.

Jason sighed. Obviously he'd asked too much. He couldn't expect her to tell him all her secrets. Not yet, anyway. He straightened up and looked around at the road, the beach, the moon on the water. He should call a cab to take him home. He should leave these vampires to themselves.

'Are you coming or not?' Sienna asked, her voice like velvet in the night.

Who was he kidding? Let Sienna drive off by herself? Comical. As if he could keep away from her.

'Yeah, I'm coming.' Jason opened the door and climbed in beside her.

As she pulled out into the California night, he smiled to himself. When he left Michigan, he'd been hoping for less of the ordinary, and more of the unexpected. Malibu had delivered in style.

So had Sienna Devereux.

If you enjoyed **BLOODLUST**,

do look out for

VAMPIRE BEACH: INITIATION

in stores from September

Read an exclusive
extract here!

VAMPIRE BEACH: INITIATION

'Hey, Freeman! Wait up!'

Jason Freeman grinned as his friend Adam's voice carried across the wide-open courtyard of DeVere High. He turned, and found himself staring into a camera lens. Adam Turnball jogged toward him, jostling his ever-present camcorder as he filmed.

'I haven't been getting the hand-held camera effect I want in my film,' Adam explained. 'The camera's not shaking enough, so I'm thinking I must walk very smoothly. I'm extremely graceful, you know.'

'Hence the jogging?' Jason asked.

'Yeah.' Adam turned off the camera and bent over, sucking in a long breath. 'I tell you, bro, I suffer for my art. Running is not my strongest subject.'

Jason chuckled. He rarely understood what Adam was talking about, but he always found the guy amusing. 'I don't even think that thing's switched on half the time,' he teased him. 'You've been making this movie ever since I met you and so far, apart from some party footage, I haven't seen squat.'

Adam fell into step beside Jason as they made their way toward the parking lot with the rest of the juniors and seniors who could drive. 'Let me guess: you think I use the camera as a shield between myself and the harsh realities of high school society. That I don't feel safe without a camera. That I'm only comfortable viewing the world at a distance, through a sanitizing camera lens.'

'No, actually, I think you just like to freak people out by pretending to film them all the time,' Jason replied.

'Damn, you got me.' Adam grinned. 'But you know I always like footage of you. The Michigan farm boy wholesomeness, the all-American blond good looks. Why, you could be the next Brad Pitt, my friend.'

'I've never set foot on a farm in my life,' Jason said. 'I'm from a suburb of Detroit.'

'Details.' Adam waved his hand dismissively in the air, his hazel eyes twinkling.

As they passed through the tall arch over the entrance to DeVere High, Jason took in a lungful of the warm California air. The scent of flowers mingled with the smell of the ocean half a mile away. Sometimes he still couldn't believe he lived in Malibu now. It had been several months, but the place hadn't lost its ability to wow him. 'I can't believe it's

223

November and I'm still wearing Tevas,' he commented. 'Do you have any idea how cold it is in Michigan right now?'

'Too cold for me,' Adam said. 'Anything below sixty-five qualifies as freezing as far as I'm concerned.'

'Hey, Freeman,' Brad Moreau called as they passed him. 'Turnball.'

'What's up?' Adam replied.

Jason nodded at Brad, his best friend on the swim team. But he didn't head over to the carved stone bench where Brad sat. Because Brad wasn't alone; he had Zach Lafrenière with him. And Zach was radiating 'no humans allowed' vibes that could probably be felt on Mars.

'What's with the vampire conference?' Adam asked, lowering his voice. 'Something going down I should know about?'

'You shouldn't know about any of it,' Jason muttered. 'And neither should I.' That was the single most astonishing thing about Malibu so far: the fact that the coolest kids in school weren't your usual 'cool' kids. In fact, they took 'cool' to a whole new level!

They were vampires.

Most days, Jason expected to wake up and realize that half his new friends being vampires was just a bizarre dream. But so far it hadn't happened. Adam was the only other person he knew who understood the truth about Zach, Brad and the rest of that posse. And Adam didn't seem to find it nearly as freaky as Jason did.

But then, Adam had grown up with the vampires. And Jason had only met them a few months ago. Maybe over time, he'd get used to knowing such a massive secret. Maybe.

'Let's just go,' he said gruffly, wanting to change the subject. The way Zach looked at him made him nervous. Of all the vampires, Zach was the only one who put Jason on edge. The others mostly acted like normal – normal for SoCal – people. But Zach was different. More powerful. More reserved. And definitely more unwilling to befriend Jason – or probably any human.

'Aren't you going to wait for Brad?' Adam asked.

Jason shook his head. 'We don't have swim practice today. Coach Middleton said since it's a holiday week, we could have the time off. He figured nobody was going to be at their best two days before Thanksgiving.'

'Sweet,' Adam said appreciatively. 'Hey, that means we can hang after school tomorrow, right? I've been meaning to force you to watch the entire *oeuvre* of Stanley Kubrick, a subject in which your knowledge is sorely lacking.'

'Hey, I've seen *The Shining*,' Jason protested.

'That's not enough,' Adam told him. 'What do you say – a DVD marathon *chez moi* tomorrow?'

'Sure,' Jason told him. They'd reached the parking lot. He nodded toward his 1975 Volkswagen Karmann Cabriolet, parked under a palm tree to the right. 'I'm that way.'

'And I remain in the bike parking section,' Adam said ruefully. 'Not that I don't love my Vespa. I just wish it had, you know, four wheels and a backseat to make out in.' He held up a fist, knuckles out toward Jason.

Jason bumped fists. 'Later.'

Adam took off for the Vespa with a wave, and Jason headed for his car. He wondered where his younger sister, Danielle, was. He'd forgotten to tell her there was no practice today. He could've driven her home. But a quick scan of the parking lot revealed no sign of Dani. She must have caught a ride or taken her usual bus.

'Guess I'm flying solo,' Jason murmured, unlocking the car. He began to lower the roof; it was way too sunny and gorgeous to ride with the top up.

'Want some help?' a voice asked from behind him.

Jason recognized that voice: *Sienna.* He felt a rush of nervous energy – *that* was just one more thing he'd got used to. Sienna Devereux made him hot, she was a vampire, and she was taken. Strangely, perhaps, he was having the most trouble with that last one.

He didn't turn around. 'I've got it, thanks,' he said.

Sienna didn't leave. He laughed and glanced over his shoulder. 'You're not really here to offer help, are you?'

'Nope,' she said, her plump lips curving into a smile. 'I'm here to ask for some. Can you give me a lift home?'

Jason finally turned to look at her full-on. Man, she was sexy. Her dark eyes were gleaming with amusement, and her long black hair was pulled into some kind of messy knot on top of her head. Jason longed to pull out the pins that held it up and let her silky hair spill down over his fingers. He shook the thoughts away. She was Brad's girlfriend. He was Brad's friend. That meant that most interesting thoughts about Sienna had to be banished from his mind.

She and I are just friends, he reminded himself. 'What's wrong with the Spider?' he asked. Sienna's imported Alfa Romeo always seemed to be out of commission.

She shrugged. 'I think it hates me.'

'That's impossible,' Jason replied. She raised one perfect eyebrow, and he realized that he sounded like a complete dork. 'Cars don't have feelings,' he added quickly. 'Unless you know something I don't.'

'I know *lots* of things you don't,' she said lightly. She opened the passenger door and folded her long legs into the VW.

'So I guess I'm giving you a ride home,' Jason laughed. He hooked the folded top into place and climbed in beside her. 'Why don't you just get a new car? Your parents have the money.'

Sienna turned in her seat to look at him. 'Really now, Michigan,' she purred. 'If I had a new car, I wouldn't need rides home, would I?'

'My point, exactly,' he told her.

She shook her head, smiling. 'Well, where would be the fun in *that*?'

Jason grinned and found himself gazing directly into her

beautiful dark eyes. Then he realized he'd been staring at her for just a bit too long.

Sienna leaned toward him. Close. So close Jason thought she was about to kiss him . . .

In fact, she gave his Michigan State key chain a casual flick with her finger. 'I think you have to use the little metal thingy on the end of this in order to make the car go,' she teased.

Jason turned the key in the ignition, trying to shake off the feeling that something had just very nearly happened between him and Sienna. 'Ha! Like you'd know,' he retorted, jokingly. 'Your car *never* goes.'

As he pulled out of the parking lot onto the Pacific Coast Highway, he caught a glimpse of Brad and Zach still sitting on the bench outside school. 'Why didn't you just wait for Brad to take you home?' he asked Sienna.

She didn't answer, and for a moment he wondered if she'd even heard him. He shot a glance at her, and she was frowning.

'He had to . . . do something with Zach,' she finally replied.

Jason nodded. It was just like he'd suspected. Brad and Zach were busy with some vampire-related business. Sienna didn't want to be specific about it, and that was OK with him. When he'd first found out about the vampires living in his gated community of DeVere Heights, he'd got pretty involved, pretty fast. One of them had turned rogue and killed a girl from school. Jason had ended up tracking him down and fighting him, all alone, in an alley. It had been that or let another girl get murdered.

If Zach Lafrenière hadn't turned up at the last moment, Jason knew he would probably have ended up dead. The whole experience had taught him everything he needed to know about the vampires: they were outrageously strong, they could change their physical appearance, and they knew some seriously freaky fighting moves.

He wasn't anxious to get that up close and personal with vampire business again. Being friends with some of them was enough – Sienna and her best friend, Belle, Brad and his oldest friend, Van Dyke. Even Zach was OK. Jason felt that they were good people and he knew their parents did a lot of charity work in the community. Beyond that, he didn't want to know much about the day-to-day vampire activities. His own private don't-ask-don't-tell policy.

A light turned red in front of him, and Jason eased to a stop. To the left, the Pacific Ocean spread out to the horizon, its gray-blue water calling to him. Maybe he'd slip on his new wetsuit and try some surfing this evening. Now that it was getting toward winter, the sun went down early. But he'd discovered that surfers stayed on the water until the very last drop of light was gone. He would definitely have time to catch a few good waves. He'd only taken three lessons so far, but he already knew enough to go out on his own.

The late afternoon sun glinted off the water, and a warm breeze ruffled his hair. It was hard to believe it was almost

Thanksgiving. Warm sun, clear blue sky, crashing ocean surf – life just did not get any better.

'You are seriously zoning,' Sienna commented.

The light was green. 'Sorry,' Jason replied, as he hit the gas. 'Sometimes the whole Malibu thing still distracts me.'

'What "whole Malibu thing"?' she asked.

'You know, the unrelenting incredibleness of the place.' That was the best way he could describe it.

'Yeah. I've been to a lot of places, and Malibu is still the most beautiful,' Sienna agreed.

Jason glanced at her in surprise. Sienna's family – in fact, all the vampire families – had more money than he could even imagine. When she said she'd been to a lot of places, he believed her. The Devereuxs vacationed in Europe, Asia, even Australia. He'd seen the photos scattered around their house. It was nice to know that California still held up, even with that kind of competition.

'Any big plans for Turkey Day?' Sienna asked as they turned off the highway and headed up the hill toward DeVere Heights.

'The usual: lots of food, football on TV,' Jason told her. 'My Aunt Bianca is coming in from New York. Danielle has about thirty outfits lined up to run by her. She approves of Bianca's fashion sense.'

'Well, who wouldn't?' Sienna said. 'The woman knows how to dress.'

Jason's eyebrows shot up. 'You know my aunt?'

'Sure.' Sienna gave a languid shrug. 'I mean, it's not like we're best friends or anything, but I've met her. Her husband was on the hospital board with my mom.'

'Oh.' Jason knew that Aunt Bianca had helped his father land his new job at the Los Angeles advertising firm – the new job with the huge raise that had led to them moving out here to Malibu. And he knew that Bianca had suggested they buy a house in DeVere Heights. But somehow he hadn't realized that Bianca knew Sienna and her parents. 'I guess Bianca's husband was really involved in all the Malibu charities and stuff, huh?' he asked.

'Yeah.' Sienna glanced over at him. 'Didn't you know that?'

'I never really thought about it,' Jason said. 'Aunt Bianca was only married to him for four years before he died. And it's not like they spent much time in Michigan – they were always off in New York or L.A. or Paris or someplace else exotic. I met him at their wedding and maybe one or twice after that.'

'So he wasn't exactly Uncle Stefan,' Sienna guessed.

'I guess he was, technically,' Jason said. 'I just never thought of him that way. We've seen a lot more of Bianca since he died than we ever did before. I think my mom is happy to have her sister back.'

'Makes sense,' Sienna said. 'But you should be glad Bianca was married to Stefan. If it wasn't for that you wouldn't be living in DeVere Heights.'

'What do you mean?'

'Bianca used his contacts. You know, pulled some strings for you guys,' Sienna explained. Then she grinned. 'We don't let just anyone live up here, you know,' she teased.

'So if it weren't for Uncle Stefan, I never would have met you,' Jason said. 'I guess I do owe him one, then.' *Was that too much?* he wondered the second the words left his mouth. Sienna always seemed to be flirting with him, but he didn't usually flirt back. He mostly figured that she was just kidding around.

Sienna didn't answer, but she gave him a long sideways look that sent the blood racing through his veins. Jason turned into the driveway of her ultra-modern house and stopped the car.

'Thanks for the ride,' she said casually, climbing out and closing the door behind her.

'No worries.' Just having her out of arm's reach made Jason relax a little. Sometimes it was hard to remember that they were only friends when she was so close by. He reached for the gearshift, but suddenly Sienna turned back to the car.

'Did I drop a pen in there?' she asked, leaning in over the door. Her hair, loosened by the wind on the drive, slipped out of its knot and fell forward around her face.

Jason's pulse sped up. *Friends!* he thought. *Who am I kidding?* She was searching the seat, but she soon found her pen and looked up. Jason stared at her lips, slightly parted, then raised his eyes to meet hers. She held his gaze and didn't move away. Without meaning to, Jason found himself leaning toward her . . .

His lips were barely an inch from hers when the phone rang.

Jason jumped in surprise as a Backstreet Boys song played out from his cell. 'Dani's idea of humor,' he explained to Sienna. 'She's always changing the ring.' He dug in the front pocket of his jeans and eventually managed to extract his phone, but he didn't recognize the number on the screen. He hit 'Talk'. 'Hello?' he barked into the mouthpiece. This was the worst-timed call he'd ever had.

It was too late. At the other end the caller had already hung up. Jason shrugged and turned back to Sienna.

But she was gone.